HALF MOON LAKE

Steve Brock

Copyright © 2022 Steve Brock

All rights reserved. No portion of this book may be reproduced in any form without permission from the publisher, except as permitted by U.S. copyright law.

For permissions contact: steve@brocknovels.com.

ISBN-13:978-0-578-39197-7

Despite my objections as a grade school kid who wanted to play outside, my mom wouldn't allow that until I had practiced reading and writing for her each day. I hated doing it sometimes, but now I know she was helping me create a solid foundation upon which I could build a higher education and career.
Thanks, Mom, I dedicate this book to you.
I wish you were here to read it.

I give Special thanks to
Tona P. and Amy.

My undying gratitude goes to fellow author, Hannah Alexander.

Chapter 1

What would it be today? Indigo, purple, or maybe some shade of green? It was something he had grown to appreciate, even anticipate during the last few years. Depending on the season and the hour of the day, the color of the water in Half Moon Lake changed. Ripples on the surface glistened and danced in the sunlight as he approached from the east. Billowy cotton-ball clouds floated high against the evening sky. Pine trees, majestic and tall, surrounded the lake. They seemed to stretch to touch the belly of the plane.

He lingered one last moment to admire the vista, but eventually keyed the mic.

"TC8750 to Half Moon Flight Service."

The familiar voice of Rose Larson broke a few seconds of static. "This is Half Moon. Is that you, Crease Williams? I hope this is an obscene radio call." No one ever accused Rose of ridged formality.

"I'm afraid it's all business today, Rose. I'm here to pick

up the floatplane to fly a load of supplies up to that group of fishermen at Roudy's Cabin."

"Fishermen? Do you mean those four CEO types who were through here last week? I saw the list of supplies they ordered. I don't know about the fishing, but it appears the beer drinking is going pretty well up there. The runway's clear, Crease."

To call what serves to land small airplanes a runway was generous. A strip along the side of the lake a quarter mile long and maybe one hundred feet wide, it was a grass field dozed free of trees and rolled to flatten some humps. Crease coaxed his little Cessna to the north, taking a wide loop to a course parallel with the landing strip.

Just as he was straightening his heading, pointing the nose toward the windsock that stood just past the end of the landing field, his life changed. At once there was deafening silence and a violent lurch downward. The engine had stopped, and he thought he must have dropped at least five hundred feet. A quick glance at the altimeter said no, but his testicles said yes.

A dozen thoughts fought for attention in his mind. He filtered through the "whys" and concentrated on the one thought that mattered: *How do I land a plane without power?* He knew it could be done. *The space shuttle always lands without power,* he thought to himself. Sure, that's right. Of course, an astronaut pilots the shuttle, not a washed-out wide receiver with a few hundred hours of flight time. Still, he believed he could do it, and it wasn't like he had a lot of options.

Just as he had convinced himself, the plane jerked forward as the engine started running again. It appeared that his heading was fairly correct, and the desire to touch the ground overwhelmed the urge to swing the plane around to line up perfectly. He eased it down and, with a bit of a hop, came into contact with the grass. He taxied forward, slowing, and came to a stop at the end of the landing area. He sat motionless until his mind and his gonads agreed he was on the ground.

Crease climbed the three steps to the single door that opened into the small reception area that was also the Half Moon radio room. As he walked through the door, an office chair swung around and a well-nourished fortysomething lady sporting a bouffant hairstyle stood. With a big toothy grin, Rose said, "There you are, you big linebacker. Come here and give me a hug."

"Just try and stop me," he said as he met her in front of the desk. As they embraced he said, "You know I was never a linebacker. In fact, I tried to avoid them as much as possible."

"Hell, Crease, all football players are linebackers to me. What have you been up to? I haven't seen you in a coon's age."

"I've been down in Texas doing some maintenance on the home place. Which reminds me, I think I might have something for you here in my duffel bag." He didn't know everything about Rose. She was divorced twice that he knew of, and scuttlebutt was that at least one settlement was enough to set her up for life. He got the feeling the only reason she helped out around the field was because she was lonely. He liked her. The truth was, he was closer to Rose than anyone since the accident. "While I was home, I picked up a little something for you." He reached into his bag and produced a two-pound box of Pangburn's Millionaires.

Her smile increased as he handed her the box. "Are you trying to wreck my perfect figure?"

"God, no. It looks to me like you're down a few pounds.

I don't want you to dry up and blow away."

"You're just oozing that old Southern charm, darlin'. How is it no one has claimed you yet?"

"I guess the bad outweighs the good. I'm not much for long-term relationships. How have you been?"

"I'm still walking upright so I can't complain." Rose returned to her chair, clutching the box of chocolate turtles.

Since he had moved up north, Rose was as close to a friend as he had. After losing his family and discovering he had no future, he determined he would maintain a certain distance from people. He had become a loner, and it suited him now. Rose was almost an exception.

He rested his hands on the counter. "Is Ol' Pete around?"

"He's here someplace. Walk through the showroom to the garage, and you'll find him."

With genuine concern, he asked, "Are you okay? Seriously, you look tired."

"It's nothing. I've not been sleeping well lately."

"I'm planning to be around for a while, so I'm gonna keep an eye on you."

"That just makes my day. Would you like for me to page Pete for you?"

"Nah, I'll head back to the garage as you said. I'll come across him."

"You know you're not exactly his favorite person, right?"

"Yeah, I remember. I'm not sure what I ever did to make him dislike me so much."

"You know what you did."

Crease did know. It wasn't like he destroyed an aircraft. It could have happened to anyone learning to land a floatplane. Anybody with limited experience could bring a plane down a bit too hard. Yes, the hard landing on the water ruptured a float, and yes, the fuselage took on a lot of water, and yes, they had to use a come-along to drag the plane into shore. The bottom line was that the plane got repaired, and he had paid for it, every cent. That should be enough for any reasonable person, but Ol' Pete wasn't altogether reasonable. He had an unnatural attachment to his floatplanes. Three years later now, and Pete still hadn't forgiven him for that little faux pas.

He had apologized, and he had learned his lesson, but that had little impact on Ol' Pete. Pete had grown up around airplanes. His dad flew them, repaired them, and even created them. He had taught Pete everything there was to know about single-engine aircraft: what made them fly, and what made them crash. If there was anyone in the world who could make a bowling ball fly, it was Pete. By the same token, if anybody could explain why an almost new Cessna TTX, well maintained and treated with care, would suddenly decide to shut down on approach, that, too, would be Pete.

Following Rose's direction, he began walking through the warehouse, toward the garage. The warehouse was a local wonder. Around here, if you wanted to do some shopping in a national chain big box store, you were in for a big disappointment. The closest Walmart was over one hundred miles away. The closest thing to that was the warehouse of the Half Moon Airfield and Wilderness Outfitters. Not that it compared to a big box store in ambiance. There was no nicely tiled floor or rows of pristine shelves stacked with goods. The "Outfitters," as it was locally known, was a large open building with a bare concrete floor stacked with pallets. It was filled with anything useful in camping, fishing, hunting, or any other outdoor activity. Beyond the warehouse and to the right stood the door to the garage. He cringed a little as he rounded the corner.

He hated to ask Pete for anything. Every conversation they had since the "incident" always began the same way. Ol' Pete sat behind an old metal office desk stained and dented by years of use and abuse. His feet were propped up as he leaned back in his rickety old wooden chair. On his head was the only hat he'd ever seen Pete wear. Ragged and stained with years of head sweat, it was adorned with hooks and fishing lures all around. Sure as spring rain, as if reading from a script, Pete said, "Well, well, if it ain't the local football star. Sink any floatplanes lately?" He always followed that statement with a snicker. That was what Crease hated the most, the snicker.

Over the last couple of years, he had learned to take a beat before continuing the conversation. Deep down, Crease knew Ol' Pete didn't really hate him. Pete wasn't that kind of person. Pete loved his planes like family, and his harassment at the start of every encounter was Ol' Pete's way of reminding Crease that the "incident" was not forgotten.

The truth was that Pete liked Crease a lot, despite the "incident." Crease had become one of the better pilots he knew. He realized Crease had some rough times in his past and he respected him for coming through it and creating a new life for himself. He figured he would stop harassing Crease about the "incident" soon. Just not today.

After a brief, pregnant pause, Crease answered the sarcastic question with a humble response, "No," he said with a weak smile, "I've learned my lesson."

"Glad to hear it. So what brings you to our little neck

of the woods?"

"I flew in to pick up a load of supplies for the campers up at Roudy's Cabin."

"Surely you didn't come to see me about a beer run."

"I did not. When I was making my approach today, I had problems with the Cessna."

"What kind of problem?"

"It just stopped running. That's an issue I haven't seen before. There was no warning. One second it was running just fine, and the next second it just quit. Have you ever seen anything like that before?"

Ol' Pete took a drag from the cheap cigar he was smoking, then took it out of his mouth and said, "Can't say that I have, not without some symptoms first. Even then, engines don't just stop completely. Did you put gas in it?"

Crease wasn't sure if that was supposed to be funny or not, so he didn't answer the question directly. "I checked everything before I took off this morning."

"Did you land it without power?"

"No, that's another odd thing. It started up again all on its own a few seconds later."

"That's odd all right, and kinda hard to believe."

That comment did not surprise Crease. He had a hard time believing it himself. "Would you have time to look at it while I'm making my run?"

Ol' Pete drew another long puff on his cigar, laid it down on the ashtray and finally replied, "Yeah, I'll give it a once-over."

"I appreciate that, Pete. Do you want me to bring it up here to the garage?"

"Nah, leave it where it is. I may take it up for a little cruise around the lake."

"Thanks, Pete, I'll check in with you when I get back."

Crease headed back into the warehouse area and told one of the warehouse guys, Little Al, he was called, what he was there for. In about fifteen minutes, he was looking at a small pallet stacked with the supplies he was to deliver to Roudy's Cabin. Mostly food items, including steaks, lobster, Crown Royal, and imported beer among assorted other items. The people who rented Roudy's Cabin were not known for living on the cheap.

After he had confirmed everything was there, Al got an electric pallet lift and took the supplies out to the dock. Crease stopped by the office, got the keys to one of the floatplanes, and led his helper to load it. He did his preflight check and climbed into the pilot's seat.

Taking off in a floatplane gives you a different feeling than taking off from a runway. The spray picked up by the prop and the gentle bobbing up and down in the water make you feel like you are driving a boat. Then, as you gain speed and the floats began to lift out of the water, you become a pilot again. It is a unique feeling that most people, even pilots, never experience. It was something Crease had come to appreciate.

The wings of a floatplane are set farther off the ground than land-based planes like his Cessna TTX. That gives them the ability to climb more steeply and turn sharper, attributes that are necessary when taking off from the surface of a small lake and clearing the surrounding trees. It was only a thirty-minute flight to Roudy's Cabin. He could make the entire trip at one thousand feet if he wanted to. From that altitude, he could sometimes see herds of deer or elk in the openings in the tree line.

The job paid well, but that wasn't why he chose it. He chose this life because his old one had died, and this was as far away from being a Texas football player as anything he could think of. That and it gave him a sense of freedom that he'd never had before, and freedom was something he needed very badly right now.

The sun still hung high in the sky as he approached Roudy's Cabin. He brought the plane down, and gently, ever so gently, touched the floats down on the surface of the lake. He pulled it over and nudged the frame up against the dock.

Floatplanes aren't particularly loud, as planes go, but out here in the wilderness where the closest automobile is over fifty miles away, it normally gets people's attention. Usually, someone comes down and helps anchor the plane to the dock. He could do it and had occasionally, but it was unusual.

He walked up to the utility shed positioned not far from the end of the dock. He retrieved the ATV from within, hooked up the small trailer, and drove it down to the plane. He off-loaded all the supplies onto the trailer, climbed aboard the ATV, and headed toward the cabin.

Despite the image conjured by the name, Roudy's Cabin was neither rowdy nor a cabin. The style of the structure could best be described as "rustic elegance." Sitting just fifty yards from the water's edge, the cabin was a well-appointed, 5,500-square-foot structure with five bedrooms, four baths, two fireplaces, and a game room complete with a billiard table and wet bar. The kitchen, with a full complement of professional-grade appliances, was the envy of every chef who saw it. The whole building was surrounded by a twelve-foot covered porch furnished with chaise lounges, rockers, a built-in grilling station, and a whirlpool tub. It was definitely constructed for leisure living.

The forest had been cleared all around the cabin, stumps removed, and a nice stand of grass nurtured to grow. Most people who stayed in the cabin probably never adventured beyond its lawn. The exception was those who wanted to hunt moose or elk. There were several places much better for that, however, so die-hard hunters rarely stayed here. Most people who used the cabin wanted to get out of the city and "get back to nature," at least as long as nature came with five-star accommodations.

It was for that reason that it was unusual for Crease not to be met at the dock upon arrival. He thought perhaps they were grilling out back of the cabin, and since the back entrance led into the kitchen, where most of the supplies should go, he slowly drove around the cabin to the grilling station.

Finding no one, he shut off the ATV and just listened for a moment. He thought perhaps he would hear music or the TV from inside the house, but there was nothing but the sounds of nature around him. He picked out a couple of bags of frozen items and headed to the double doors. The doors were unlocked, but there was nothing unusual about that.

Out here, the visitors who showed up in the middle of the night would not turn the doorknob. Other than the residents of the cabin, there were probably no other human beings within twenty square miles. There were plenty of other creatures milling around in the dark. Raccoons, possums, skunks, foxes, and rabbits were always looking for any food scraps that might be left out. Those critters, as Rose called them, could be a bit of a nuisance, but not dangerous.

There were dangers in the north woods, but nothing was likely to break through the door. The most obvious concern, if you asked people, would be bears and wolves. Certainly, both species were present in the woods around the cabin, but black bears were shy around humans, and grizzlies didn't inhabit the area. A pack of wolves could certainly ruin your day, but only if you presented yourself as a weak or wounded target.

What surprised most people was learning that the most dangerous animals in the area were elk and moose. Not that either is aggressive by nature, but many people who have never seen them don't respect their space. The problem comes when people approach elk expecting Rudolph, but what they find are charging, pointed antlers propelled by a bristled, snorting, seven hundred pounds of pissed-off.

Crease walked through the door into the kitchen. He deposited the frozen items in the large freezer. He went about unloading the rest of the supplies, being intentionally loud, hoping to draw attention to his presence. With the last bag delivered, he stood silently for a moment. The beautiful house felt more like a derelict, abandoned mansion. It was creepy-silent.

He decided to do a walk-through to make sure no one was around. Walking room to room he found the same, a house that could have been a college dormitory, in desperate need of a maid. There was no question guys had been living here, but they weren't here now. In one of the bedrooms, he found a journal. Someone's musing about daily happenings. He knew it was personal, and he hated to read it, but maybe if he just peeked a little, he might discover what they'd been doing.

He decided to start with the previous day and only go as far as necessary to find a clue. He didn't have to read any further. There was an entry that said the group had been doing some hiking through the woods, and yesterday they came across something interesting. All it said was they wanted to explore it further, but the daylight was fading so they came back to the cabin. They thought they might go back to continue tomorrow.

Crease gladly closed the book, he felt like he was a peeping tom as it was. They were probably traipsing through the woods at this very moment. The creepy feeling kind of went away as he made his way out of the cabin and back to the ATV. He drove back down to the dock, put the ATV back in the shed, and climbed into the plane. Looking at that journal made him feel better, but he would keep it to himself.

Chapter 2

Crease landed the floatplane with caution that would make Ol' Pete proud. He wasn't sure Pete would have had the time to take a look at the Cessna, but he was hopeful.

He stopped at the office long enough to drop off the floatplane key, then walked back to the garage to find Pete. It took a while. Pete wasn't in the garage and no one was sure where to find him. Crease noticed the Cessna had moved since he'd been gone so he walked out to take a look.

When Crease found him, he was in the pilot's seat, in a manner of speaking. Pete was inverted, head and shoulders in the floorboard, legs and feet dangling over the cushion. Seeing Ol' Pete in that position presented a bit of a quandary. On one hand, Crease hated to disturb him in the middle of what Crease had asked him to do. Perhaps it would be better to walk away quietly and find him later. On the other hand, however, in all the years he had known Ol' Pete, he had never seen him without a cigar and Crease was curious to know if a person could smoke one while being upside down.

Curiosity won out. "Hey, Pete, have you found anything?"

Ol' Pete, a bit startled by the question, leaned his head to look up at Crease, took the cigar out of his mouth, and replied, "Yeah, I found something. I found that you have a sweet little ride here. I gave her the once-over twice, then I took her up for a test flight. I flew her hard, made her climb, dove her, banked her sharp, hell I even did a couple of barrel rolls. She never missed a beat. There ain't nothin' wrong with this airplane. After testing everything, the only thing I can come up with that might have caused the problem is…"

Crease knew what he was going to say, so he joined him in unison as they both said, "Pilot error."

Pete continued. "I only say that because she's working just fine now. Look, son, I don't believe you caused her to shut down. I don't know how you could do that without knowing it. So unless you are jerkin' my chain about the whole thing, I'm stumped."

"I wouldn't make up something like that. If you've already checked everything and can't find a problem, what are you doing now?"

"I don't like mysteries when they involve aircraft. For the last few months I've been working on a little device, kind of like the black box that is installed in jet planes, except I've made this one specifically for small, single props like this one. I'm installing it now. I didn't figure you'd mind."

"No, not at all. You think this little device will track down the problem?"

"It will record everything that happens while in flight. If the plane shuts down again, it should tell us why, or at least give us something to go on. It's not as indestructible as a black box, though. If you have another issue like before, and you don't land it in one piece, it won't survive the crash. Of course, you probably won't either." Ol' Pete chuckled to himself. "Give me another fifteen minutes and you can have her. When you take her up, just fly like you always do and forget the little device is even there."

Crease was a little disappointed that Pete couldn't find anything that might have caused the problem. It made him doubt his own experience, could he have imagined it? No, no, he hadn't, but maybe it was one of those fluke occurrences that defy explanation. It'll probably never happen again.

November 13, 2010, was a day that began with a great deal of promise and anticipation. It didn't end that way. By the time he was a sophomore wide receiver for Texas Christian University, he had already been noticed by one or two local NFL scouts.

Toby Williams had the size, the speed, and the quick and sure hands necessary for a quality NFL receiver. The final piece of the puzzle, the X factor, became apparent during that sophomore year. Toby could locate the weak point in an opponent's defense, the spot in a zone coverage that lay between a linebacker's zone and that of a cornerback. The place where knowing who was responsible to cover him was unclear. His wide receiver coach called that spot the "crease" in the secondary. A wide receiver who could find it, feel it really, could make himself a wide-open target for his quarterback. His ability to consistently do this resulted in his coach beginning to call him Crease. After a while, his teammates followed suit and soon his entire world knew him as Crease Williams.

That Saturday TCU was hosting San Diego State. It was a big game. It was common knowledge there would be NFL scouts in attendance. On top of that, the Horned Frogs had a good record that season and a win would go a long way toward being invited to a bowl game.

As important as all that was, Crease had a personal motivation to perform well in that game. When he was a high school player, his mom couldn't have been more supportive of him. She attended all of his football games. Regardless of the weather, she could be found in the stands cheering her heart out. The truth was, however, she was never a football fan. She was a Toby Williams fan, a mother's son fan.

When he got to college and decided to play football there, too, she told him that he was a grown man now, and grown men didn't need their mom at every game. It had bothered him, but he told her he understood. So during his college football career, his dad attended almost every home game, but rarely his mom.

A few days before this game, this big game, this game that could potentially launch his NFL career, she told him she was planning to attend. She said she kept hearing people say what a great player he had become, and she didn't doubt it, but she wanted to experience it for herself.

All these factors added up to a substantial amount of pressure going into the game. For many people that pressure could be debilitating. There are many examples of people succumbing to pressure in sports history. For Crease, though, it just didn't factor into his thinking. Any time the team had its back against the wall, facing long yardage and short time, Crease's response would be, "Throw it to me. I'll catch it." That attitude didn't come from arrogance or self-centeredness. He had been reared to have neither of those personality traits. It came from the calmness of mind, and an unwavering belief in his abilities.

With the game on the line, down 33 to 35, and less than thirty seconds on the game clock, the quarterback threw him the ball. At the ten-yard line, he outleaped the defensive back, caught the ball, broke a tackle, and crossed the goal line. Final score: San Diego State 35, TCU 40.

The stadium erupted in pandemonium. The marching band was playing excitedly, trying desperately to be heard over the din. The student body collectively stormed onto the field. His teammates jumped and yelled, arms in the air, then hugged one another. A few of them grabbed a cooler filled with ice and sports drink and poured it all over the head coach from behind. Crease joined in the revelry but also looked to find his parents in the stands. His eyes met theirs, and although they were still fifty yards apart, he could see that they were beaming with pride. He had finished the game with 187 yards receiving and scored three touchdowns.

As he fought his way through the crowd, an NFL scout stopped and congratulated him, and said they would be seeing a lot of each other. When finally he got to his parents, his dad threw an arm around his neck and told him how proud he was. His mom embraced him and said, "Now I see what everybody was talking about." He felt a great sense of accomplishment. As they stood there together, several family friends came to offer their congratulations as well. It would have been the greatest day of his life if it had ended there, but it hadn't.

When the congratulations began to trail off, Crease told his parents the team was getting together for a celebration. He embraced each of them one last time and told his mom how happy he was that she came to the game. Finally, he said he wouldn't be out late and he would see them at home. Despite his sincerity, however, he would not.

Jacob and Ruth watched as their son walked away. He hadn't gotten far before he was mauled by a group of teammates. There would be partying, no doubt, but they weren't concerned. Toby had shown himself to be quite responsible.

The couple turned away and started the long walk back to their Acadia. Jacob reached out and took Ruth's hand. They walked for quite a while without conversation. They were both replaying the game in their minds. Finally, they came to section D4, where they had parked before the game.

As they approached the SUV Jacob reached into his pocket and retrieved the key fob. He double-clicked the unlock button and asked Ruth, "Would you like to drive? It's your vehicle."

"No, you drive. I'm kinda worn out."

She walked around to the passenger side and he got in behind the wheel. He had to adjust everything: the distance to the pedals, the tilt of the steering wheel, the height of the seat, and so forth until he got it ready for him to drive. She had driven to the stadium and she liked everything to be set a certain way. She wouldn't have any trouble putting things back. There was a driver preset button she had programmed with her settings. It was her vehicle for sure, but not just because of the preset button, and not just because her name was on the title.

They had married young. Too young, according to most anyone you talked to at the time. They ignored those naysayers. They were in love and that would be enough. Toby was born just about a year after the wedding. They never went hungry, but they lived paycheck to paycheck for several years.

Jacob had been aware that Ruth's childhood had been filled with hard times. She had told him stories of the way she lived as a child and it broke Jacob's heart to hear it. He vowed to himself to provide Ruth with everything she wanted.

As the years passed, he worked hard and made good decisions with money. Two years ago money was no longer a concern. Not that they were wealthy, but they owned the home they lived in and had enough money in retirement accounts to let them live comfortably.

When it became necessary to buy a new vehicle, Jacob was not going to be dissuaded from getting exactly what Ruth wanted. She had always admired GMC vehicles equipped with the Denali trim package. She liked the Acadia for its size and utility ability. She wanted a champagne color and it was important for it to have a heads-up display.

They both searched for weeks until finally, they found an Acadia in the right color that was a Denali, equipped with a heads-up display. It made Jacob very happy to buy it for her. Jacob drove it sometimes, but it was her vehicle.

It took quite a while to drive out of the parking lot and across the bridge to the highway on-ramp. They crept along in bumper-to-bumper traffic doing fifteen miles per hour. The other side of the highway was moving at normal highway speed. Jacob knew the congestion they were in was only because of stadium traffic. Five miles ahead they would cross the 273 interchanges. They would lose half this traffic after that, and then they would speed up. They should be home in less than an hour.

Jacob expected Ruth to be asleep by this time, but she

was still looking out the side window. He could tell she had something on her mind. She made small talk for a while and after a brief silence she looked toward Jacob and said, "He is good, isn't he?" It was as much a statement as a question. He took it to require an answer.

"He's more talented than I ever imagined he could be."

"He'll be okay, won't he? This NFL interest in him won't change him, make him arrogant or uppity?"

Again Jacob answered what could have been a statement. "He's got plenty of reason right now to be full of himself, and he isn't. Face it, Momma, you did a good job teaching him humility."

That comment made her smile. "It was a team effort."

"I'm happy to take part of the credit."

With that, the conversation ended, but he could tell Ruth still had something to say. After twenty years of marriage, he had learned to read her very well. He was pretty sure he knew what was on her mind.

He was right. After a few moments of silence, Ruth, looking not at him, but directly forward, said, "I wish he hadn't taken that test."

He knew what she really meant was, I wish you hadn't suggested he take that test. He appreciated her diplomatic approach, trying not to place blame. He already blamed himself enough for both of them. The reality was no one was to blame. The test didn't cause any problems. It just revealed them. They would have revealed themselves in time, test or not.

"Are you going to tell him you got the report this week?" Ruth asked.

"Not just now, I want to let him enjoy his moment in the sun. There's no hurry. There will be plenty of time to talk about it after the bowl game. After the win today I'm sure the team will get an invitation."

As he waited to hear her response a feeling came over him. It was a sense of danger. Something was very wrong, but what? At the moment they were sitting still. He looked ahead but saw nothing except car after car as far as the horizon. He looked at Ruth, and she was sitting calmly. It didn't matter. The feeling persisted.

He checked the rearview mirror but again saw car after car behind them, all sitting stationary. He was about to say something to Ruth when, in his peripheral vision, he saw movement. It was in the grass median between the two halves of the highway, where there shouldn't be anything but grass. He turned to look left, and there it was. The sight froze him as he watched it. An object was moving across the grass, rapidly coming toward them. It was a truck, a big eighteen-wheeler. It was barreling forward, bounding up and down as it crossed the uneven ground, looking like a living monster as it grew closer by the second.

Instinctively his first impulse was to hit the brake, but he was already holding the brake. They were sitting still. There was no time. *You have to move*, a voice in his head screamed. *MOVE!* Operating on impulse he moved his foot off the brake and mashed the accelerator. The Acadia lunged forward, but only for an instant. It slammed into the rear of the car in front of them and the airbags deployed, knocking them both back in their seat. The bags deflated immediately and for an instant, he could see Ruth's heads-up display. It read zero as the windshield shattered. The driver's door caved in as the monster arrived.

Two seconds of violence gave way to calm. Ruth tried to call his name. "J...Ja...Jacob?" She wasn't sure she had actually made a sound, "J...Jacob?"

21

She was vaguely aware of sounds around her. Hissing. Someone screaming in the distance...

Sounds again, voices...closer this time...

She became aware of something sharp against her chest. She couldn't see it—her eyes wouldn't work. She thought maybe...

Voices, talking now. "Are they...you know...Oh my God." The voices faded...She felt warm all over...

A light. She saw a light, growing larger, brighter.

She smelled apple pie.

Chapter 3

Spirits were understandably high after the San Diego State game. Everyone was excited at the possibility of a bowl game invitation. There was always a crowd gathered at the Frog Pond after a football game. The Frog Pond is the favorite eating and drinking establishment for the team and its supporters. This Saturday the bar and grill was packed.

Crease drank a couple of beers with his teammates and danced with a couple of pep squad members. When it came to members of the fairer sex, Crease was as interested as any college-aged guy. He had dated regularly in high school, but when he got to college, between football practices, games, and other team obligations, he found it was all he could do to keep his grades up without a lot of dating. He figured he would have years after school to find the right girl to spend his life with, but he would have just this one chance to do well and graduate with a degree.

He dated some, usually for college-sponsored events,

but for the most part, he was content to focus on what he saw as the important things at this time in his life. That meant doing well at college classes and performing well on the football field. He knew there was a good chance of having a professional football career, and he welcomed that opportunity. He wasn't counting on it, however. He knew there were no guarantees, and the possibility of a career-ending injury was a real concern. So while he worked hard to impress the football scouts, he worked just as hard to maintain a good GPA. That would be his safety net, should one be necessary.

He knew his sense of responsibility was something his mom and dad had instilled in him growing up, and he knew they were proud of him for the way he approached college. He didn't do it for them. He was glad they approved, but he did it for himself. He wanted to have as many options in life as possible with the opportunities that were open to him. He didn't see that as selfish; he felt it was simply pragmatic.

The Frog Pond was nothing fancy. It had been around since the 1960s and it may still be using the original decor. It featured a U-shaped bar surrounded by tables of various sizes along with a game room with a couple of pool tables and old pinball machines.

Crease mingled through the crowd on his way to the bar. He walked up next to Tyrone Bevee, ordered a beer, turned toward Tyrone, and said, "Good game today, man."

Tyrone Bevee's attitude was like life owed him a dollar but only paid him a dime. Tyrone's posture stiffened a bit when he saw who had spoken. Without turning to face him, he replied, "You too. What did you end up with, like a hundred yards or something?"

"Something like that," Crease said, unwilling to correct him. "Have you got big plans after graduation?"

Bevee stiffened even more, "Something will turn up." And with that, he turned and walked through the crowd.

Tyrone Bevee was the heir-apparent before Crease came along. Tyrone was a year ahead of Crease in college, so when he lost his starting position as a senior, to a junior like Crease, it was hard to accept.

Bevee had plans for the NFL, but they were founded nowhere but his mind. He should have lost his starting position as a junior, but the coaches weren't comfortable with a sophomore as a full-time starter. This year it was too obvious who the better wide receiver was. They had to give the flanker position to Crease for the good of the team.

The bartender brought Crease the Pearl he had ordered, any true Texas boy's beer of choice. Lone Star got more marketing, but Pearl was the true Texas product. He would never get to drink this one, however. In about ten seconds his cell phone would ring, it would be the Texas Highway Patrol, and with that Crease's life would never be the same.

She hugged Crease so hard it almost hurt. Sobbing, she tried to speak through the tears. "I'm so sorry, Crease...I wish I could say something that would help. I can't even imagine how you are feeling right now."

"It's still not entirely real to me, and maybe that's a good thing. I appreciate your concern, very much." That was true. He was grateful to everyone who offered him condolences. He knew they were sincere, and they didn't know what they could do to ease his pain.

The weather was perfect, if there was such a thing for a funeral. The sun might have risen that morning, but you could barely tell. Dark clouds hung low as far as the horizon. Rain began early in the day and continued to fall softly. It wasn't stormy. There was no lightning or thunder to break the mood. The day was as mournful as a day could be.

She let go of the embrace but clutched Crease's arm with both hands. Her heart hurt for him. She knew how important his family was to him. They had dated for a while, and she thought she knew him pretty well. Her mama would have said he was a keeper. She would be right. She would have loved to take him back home to Alabama to meet her family, but that was for another time.

"Can I get you anything?" she asked him hopefully.

"Yes, some water would be good." Not that he really needed water, but he could see his coaches not far down in the line, and he needed some time to think about what he was going to say.

She slid between mourners. She had a mission and as minor as it was, it was something. He watched her walk away and wondered if she knew that at the moment, she was the closest thing to family that he had, and she was little more than a friend.

He stood alone next to the two identical closed caskets. Closed because the occupants died a violent death, and funeral directors could only do so much. It was probably for the best. He didn't need to see what rested inside. He somberly greeted each person who passed by, thanking them for coming. It was insincere gratitude, as harsh as that sounded. He was in torment. Life as he knew it was over, and there was nothing anyone could do or say to change that. Standing and greeting people politely was just what you did, what society expected of the tormented. So he did it, because he couldn't bring himself to not do it and because his mom would want him to do it. One small comfort was that it would be over soon, but the worst was yet to come.

First to console him was his wide receiver coach, a good man who genuinely cared about his players. "I don't have the words to express how sorry I am, Crease."

"I know. No one does. What could you say? I appreciate you being here."

"If I or the college can do anything, please let me know. We'll all get through this, as horrible as it is. Next year, things will be better. We will move past this. Your team will be there for you."

It was here. The moment he dreaded was at hand. "I know you mean well, but I don't think I'll be coming back to the team." What he said wasn't strictly true. He didn't just *think* he wouldn't be coming back. He absolutely wouldn't be coming back. He couldn't say that, not right now.

His coach stood in stunned silence. Finally, he composed himself and said, "Take some time, think about things. I know it's hard to think about the future right now."

"You're right, it is, but I've thought about it. Football is not my future anymore. I'm grateful to you for all the support you've given me the last three seasons, but I'm finished with football."

He could tell his coach was having trouble processing the words he was saying. Finally, the coach said, "We'll talk again later." He said it with a smile, and he believed it.

"Okay," was all Crease could muster in response, but he had no intention of discussing it again. Crease breathed a sigh of relief as the rest of the coaches gave their condolences and walked on. The rest of the line passed by slowly, but without incident. The line was long. His parents were good people and had many friends. He dutifully greeted them all, and it was the last time he would see any of them.

The house was older, but in good condition. It was more than a house to him. It was a home, the only home he had ever known. With the funeral and burial completed, he was faced with disposing of their lives. Harsh words, but that was the reality. A painful process that all survivors must go through.

He sat in his father's favorite chair, taking in the sight of so many memories. The sofa where he sat on countless Sundays, watching football with his dad. The china hutch, full to overflowing with little figurines that his mom called faceless angels. How many occasions had he searched for a new one, one she didn't have? It had gotten more difficult in the last couple of years. It seemed she had them all. He'd look anyway, and he had always found something new. He didn't know if they were valuable; they were valuable to her, and so they were priceless to him.

His mom devoted one shelf in the hutch to the china that belonged to his grandma. His mom only got it out for Thanksgiving and Christmas dinners. He had eaten from those plates exactly twice a year since he could remember.

Everywhere he looked, he found a memory. These things didn't belong to him. Yes, everything had been left to him in the will, but these things were theirs. The memories were his.

He couldn't sell anything, wouldn't sell anything. He'd leave it just as it is, as they left it. He couldn't stay here anymore. It hurt too much. He wasn't sure just where he'd go or what he would do, but it would be as far from Fort Worth, Texas, and football as he could get. That much he knew.

There were things to be done before he could go. A small leak above the range in the kitchen needed to be fixed, and the house needed a fresh coat of paint. He'd take care of those things before he left.

The last thing he had to do, now that the funeral was over, was to find the important papers. That's what his dad called them. The papers that document a person's or couple's life, those things the government would want him to have. His dad had talked about them from time to time. There was no safe in the house. His dad had always talked about getting one but never got around to doing it.

There was a metal lockbox in the bedroom closet. He was sure that was where he'd find what he needed. It didn't take long to find the box and the key. He opened the box and thumbed through the papers; last year's income tax report, property tax receipts, a copy of the will, all the things he was looking for, and one that he wasn't.

It was an envelope from the laboratory where his father had sent his DNA for testing. His father felt it was a good idea to have test results to provide to NFL teams who might be interested in drafting him out of college. DNA testing wasn't being required, but his dad thought it would keep him one step ahead of other collegiate players. He didn't care; it was no big deal to him, but if his dad thought it was important, then it was fine.

The envelope was postmarked a couple of weeks ago. Why had his dad not mentioned it? He remembered providing the sample several months ago. His dad told him it would take a long time to receive results. Here it was and his dad had not said a word.

It was a long-winded report that included a lot of technical terms he didn't understand. He finally came to one paragraph that made him realize why his dad had said nothing. He supposed his dad hadn't found the words yet before he was killed. He read the paragraph again, to be sure he understood what it was saying. He did.

In the SMU game his sophomore year, he had taken a hit from a linebacker that knocked him unconscious for a moment. When he came around, his thinking was jumbled for a while. He couldn't maintain a line of thought. That was how he felt as he read the paragraph for the second time.

Finally, he put the information away in his mind. He mentally marked it for future reference. His life was in tatters, and he had to figure out how to keep going just to get through today, and then tomorrow. The paragraph was offering information for another day. He would deal with it when the time came, not today.

He packed the envelope with all the other papers, gathered a suitcase full of his belongings, and left the house. He couldn't sleep there now. He got a hotel room where he would stay until he determined his future.

Chapter 4

The Bobcat Bar and Grill was rockin'. In the center of a raised stage that faced a collection of round wooden tables and ladder-back chairs, a middle-aged R and B diva gyrated her hips to the music. With a double-fisted death grip on a stand-up microphone, she belted out lyrics: "R-E-S-P-E-C-T...Find out what it means to me..." The stage lights created spheres of pink and blue fog in the smoke-filled atmosphere. A saxophone player swung his horn back and forth in rhythm with the music, while the keyboard player stood and pounded the keys of a baby grand piano like they insulted his sister. The diva ended the song with a flourish and the already dancing crowd erupted with applause.

The singer announced a quick break while the more intoxicated in the crowd continued to clap in appreciation. When the noise subsided, a uniformed deputy sitting at the bar looked at the keyboard player and said, "I hate to be a killjoy, but don't you think we ought to get our prisoner to the station, Sheriff?" He nodded his head toward a scruffy-looking character in handcuffs next to him.

Still smiling from the moments on stage, Sheriff Maurice Broussard replied, "Yeah, you're right, Joe. Let's pack him up and go."

As he spoke, he felt a hand on his shoulder. The sax player said, "Come back and sit in with us again, Mo."

"Count on it. I'll be back," the sheriff said with a big smile. The 10-15 call was the reason they came to the Bobcat, but Sheriff Mo couldn't resist the chance to relive his jazz band days back on Bourbon Street in a previous life.

He was a native of New Orleans, but like so many others, Katrina had forced him to flee north on a temporary relocation. At least, that was the original plan. Once here, he found some stability that he lacked before. The weather took some getting used to, but it was otherwise a nice place to live, so he decided to stay. Being county sheriff wasn't something he'd ever considered before he came here, but he found it agreed with him.

He and his deputy each grasped an arm of the scruffy-looking man and led him out the door and to the car. Obviously inebriated, the prisoner asked, "What am I being arrested for?"

Joe shook his head and said, "I've told you twice already."

"For being a drunken asshole," Mo said. "You can be an asshole, and you can get drunk, but you can't do both, not around here."

After that little verbal exchange, they drove back to the office in silence. The asshole snoozed. Upon arrival, Maurice told Joe to lock him in a cell. The sheriff walked into his office and listened to a voice mail message from earlier in the day. Rose Larson was the voice on the recording. She said there might be a problem out at Half Moon Field and asked him to call in the morning. As he jotted a note, he thought to himself, *I hope Crease didn't sink another floatplane.*

Sheriff Mo walked up the steps to the glass doors on the front of the brick building that was both the sheriff's office and county jail. As he entered the room a voice from behind the counter said, "Mornin', Sheriff. Joe said you had the Bobcat jumpin' last night."

"Joe talks too much," he replied as he opened the door to his private office.

"I just made a pot of coffee if you're interested."

Sheriff Mo grabbed his cup off his desk and walked it over to the coffee station. "Is it strong?"

"Yes sir, just the way you like it." Deputy Frank Jensen, the maker of the coffee, worked the overnight shift manning the office. He knew Sheriff Mo was grateful for a fresh pot when he came in even if he didn't say so.

Frank had been a deputy for Sheriff Mo for over five years now. He liked the sheriff a lot. Mo cared for his deputies and was a fair and reasonable man. He was a bit cranky first thing in the morning, though.

Mo took a sip of the piping hot brew and smiled. "That's a good pot, Frank. Get me the number of the Outfitters before you leave."

"Yes sir."

After Frank left for the day, the office was quiet, so Mo called Rose to find out what the problem was. After a brief encounter with the automated attendant, and selecting from a couple of menus, the phone rang and Rose Larson's familiar voice said, "Half Moon Field."

"Hey there, Rose. This is Sheriff Broussard. I got your message yesterday. What's going on?"

"Hi, Sheriff. Thanks for calling me back. Like I said in the voice mail, it's probably nothing, but we've got a group of campers that we haven't heard from and we can't contact them."

"I'm assuming that's unusual? Can you elaborate a little more?"

"Yes, there are four gentlemen in the group. They rented Roudy's Cabin for an extended stay. There's no cellular service up there, so we provide campers with a satellite phone. They are free to use it as they wish, but we ask them to contact us every other day just to let us know they are okay. They haven't called and I've tried to call the satellite phone, but no one answers. Crease delivered some supplies a couple of days ago and he said he didn't see anyone around, but everything appeared to be normal."

"I thought Crease was in Texas."

"He just got back two days ago. He flew in here and took one of the floatplanes to make the delivery."

"So when was the last time anyone saw or heard from them?"

"I guess it would have been four days ago when they ordered the supplies, or it could be five days ago. I'm not sure. I didn't talk with them."

"As you said, it's probably nothing. They may have gotten caught up in whatever they're doing and just forgot to call, and maybe your calls are just missing them. Still, it's probably something I should check on just to be sure. I'll need a ride, and if Crease was the last one up there, I might want to talk with him too. Could you see if he could meet me at the airfield and fly me and a deputy up there?"

"Sure, I can call him. What time do you think?"

"Let's shoot for two o'clock. Just let me know if that won't work."

"You got it, Sheriff. Be here at two if you don't hear from me. Thanks a lot, Sheriff. That eases my mind."

Mo hung up the phone and thought to himself, *It's probably nothing.* He walked around his desk and opened the door into the outer office. He looked at the receptionist who was just getting settled in for the day. "When Deputy Pride comes in, tell him to plan on meeting me here at one thirty, and tell him to find the B and E kit."

"Will do, Sheriff. Did someone get burgled?"

"It's probably nothing."

Deputy Pride was at the office promptly at one thirty. Sheriff Mo met him and they headed for the cruiser. Pride put the B and E kit in the back and got in the passenger seat. "Where are we headed, Sheriff?"

"We need to drive out to the Outfitters. Crease is going to fly us to Roudy's Cabin."

"Did the place get broken into?"

"No, but the campers that have been renting the place haven't been checking in like they are supposed to, and Rose said they aren't answering the satellite phone. We're going to go look around and see if we can find out what's going on."

"Okay with me, Sheriff, but it sounds like a milk run."

"Yeah, it's probably nothing, but we have to check it out."

When they got to the airfield, Crease was already there, warming up the floatplane. They packed the equipment and climbed in the plane for the brief flight up to Roudy's Cabin.

Crease brought the plane down and made a soft landing on the lake. He maneuvered the plane over to the dock, and again there was no one to meet them there. At this point, however, that was no longer a surprise. They tied the plane to the dock and Crease went to the little storage shed to get the ATV. It was exactly as he had left it. The sheriff and deputy climbed in with equipment in tow, and Crease started up toward the cabin. Crease drove around to the deck door just like he had done a few days ago.

As they were getting out of the ATV the sheriff said, "Let's all wear gloves while we are here. Until we know more about what is going on, I want to treat this cabin as a crime scene."

They all gloved up and went in the patio door, which was still unlocked. "When you were here a few days ago you brought supplies. Why don't you start by looking where you put them and see if anything has been used or moved." While the sheriff directed this instruction to Crease, he told Deputy Pride, "Go through the house. Look for anything unusual or any sign of a struggle."

Deputy Pride left the kitchen to do what he was told while Crease went to the freezer, refrigerator, and pantry to inspect the supplies he had left before. It came as no great surprise to him that everything was just where he had left it. No food had was missing, nothing unwrapped, no sign of any human activity.

He could hear Deputy Pride milling around in the game room looking for anything of interest. While he was busy, Crease walked back to the bedroom area where he had read the journal before. He thought he remembered precisely where he had left it, but he saw nothing there now. He checked the other bedrooms just in case he was misremembering, but found no journal. He had left it resting on the bed, in plain sight. It shouldn't be difficult to find.

Crease went back to the kitchen and waited while Mo and Pride both continued to look through the cabin. It wasn't long before both of them had moved their search to the bedrooms. In just a few minutes, they both came back into the kitchen.

Deputy Pride said, "I see nothing to suggest any kind of struggle. There's a lot of gear in the closets, so I doubt if they are out fishing."

"What about the supplies you brought, Crease? Has anything moved?" asked the sheriff.

"No, everything I brought is just where I left it."

"So you don't see any sign of anyone being here since your supply drop?"

"Damn it. I didn't want to say anything about it, but I found a journal in one of the bedrooms, and I don't see it now."

"What kind of journal?"

"It had a black faux-leather cover and was filled with spiral loose-leaf paper. It appeared to be someone's daily, personal diary. I found it when I was looking around after I unloaded supplies. I thought maybe it might show where they were or what they'd been doing. I only read one entry, the last one, for the day before I brought supplies. It said they had been exploring in the dense forest, and they had found something interesting. They were going to go back and investigate. I figured that was what they were doing while I was here."

"Did it say what they found or where it is?"

"No, all it said was they found something they wanted to investigate further. I felt guilty reading it, being someone's diary. I wouldn't even have mentioned it except it isn't where I left it."

"Which is where?"

Crease took them to the bedroom and pointed to the bed where he had left the journal. The sheriff told Deputy Pride to check the other bedrooms while he and Crease looked there. There was no journal.

After they had looked everywhere they could think of, the sheriff told Deputy Pride, "Pull prints from all the typical surfaces. We don't have exclusion prints from the guys renting this place, but we can at least run what we find against the known felons' database. Someone has been here, someone who didn't belong."

Pride pulled prints from countertops, handles, knobs, keypads, and anything he could think of that someone might have touched without thinking. While he did, the sheriff walked around the outside of the cabin, in a circular pattern expanding outward toward the tree line. He was looking for anything unusual or just out of place.

When they were finally ready to leave, they gathered in the kitchen to compare notes. "Is there anything you have found that suggests foul play?"

Crease and Pride both shook their heads in unison. There was nothing unusual to be found. It was as if the campers had just walked away and left everything behind. The missing journal was the only thing that even suggested someone had been here in the last two days. It made little sense to Crease. Why would someone take the journal and nothing else? Who would care about a personal journal out here in the tall trees of Minnesota? He wished he'd never seen that journal, as if that would make everything okay.

Sheriff Mo said, "We're going to need to contact the families to find out if any of them have been in communication with these guys. If they haven't, we're going to declare this an official missing person case."

Crease and Deputy Pride nodded in agreement.

Chapter 5

When he graduated from TCU, Tyrone Bevee had a bachelor's degree in criminal justice. He'd never really considered what that represented because he was going to the NFL. What degree he graduated with was just a fallback position. It didn't turn out that way. They robbed him of his chance at the NFL. Robbed by Crease Williams and the wide receiver coach who gave Crease his starting position. He had the talent, but NFL scouts don't pay attention to players who don't play every down. It wasn't his fault. He was more talented than they gave him credit for.

It was a bitter pill to swallow. When graduation was over, he took his backup plan and ran with it. He applied to the Federal Bureau of Investigation. They accepted him to their training academy, where he excelled. He tried to put his football disappointment behind him. Karma, if one believes in that, was on his side. The people who robbed him of his professional football career would pay.

Once he completed the FBI training academy, he asked to be assigned to the special projects department. There they quickly promoted him to special agent in charge of the upper Midwest region. He was good as an agent, in no small measure because of his suspicion of everyone and their motives.

It was in this capacity as SAC where karma presented him a gift wrapped up in a pretty ribbon. It came as a call he received from his assistant director at the bureau one afternoon. "Agent Bevee, this is AD Kenner. Are you aware of the situation that has developed in your district?"

"Yes sir, I am up to speed on the developments. It is an unfortunate occurrence that should never have happened."

"Yes, you are right. I need you to take control of the project personally and see that any potential issues are contained. Make use of company resources as you need them. I'm sending you the report of the situation, in case it contains information you may not have."

"Yes sir. I'll leave immediately and I'll keep you informed."

As he was en route to his destination, he took the time to read the report AD Kenner had sent him. He was familiar with the situation in general, but he didn't have names for all the people on the fringe of the issue. He couldn't believe his eyes at first when he read that Toby Williams was one person involved in a minor role. There could be many people named Toby Williams in the country, but this one came with the "also known as" designation of "Crease" Williams. He was sure there was only one of those. He would happily get involved in this project.

Deputy Jensen had called three of the families of the missing campers so far, and he tapped his foot nervously as he waited for the phone to connect a fourth time. He was pretty sure this conversation would go just like the other three, and he'd be glad when it was over.

Click. "Hello."

"Hello, may I speak with Laura Douglas?"

"This is Laura."

"Laura, this is Deputy Sheriff Frank Jensen with the Pine Valley Sheriff's Department in Minnesota."

"Minnesota? Are you sure you have the right number?"

"I believe so, ma'am. Is your husband Ed on a camping trip here in Pine Valley?"

"Oh, yes. Yes, he is. Is everything okay?"

"Well, we are having difficulty getting in touch with him and the other gentlemen he is with, and we wanted to check and see if you have heard from him in the last few days."

"No, but I wasn't expecting to. He said they would be out of cell range. What do you mean you can't get in touch with them?"

"They were given a satellite phone to use while they were at the cabin, and they had been calling to check-in until a few days ago. After they stopped checking in, we tried to call the phone and no one answers."

"Are you saying something has happened to him?"

"We don't have any reason to expect that. Right now we're just looking for information."

"Oh my God, Ed."

Frank could hear Laura sob into the phone. "Ma'am, please don't worry. We have no reason to believe anything bad has happened. They may just be off fishing and forgot to check-in. Ma'am? Ma'am?"

Still sobbing, she said, "Yes, okay."

"We'd appreciate it if you would let us know if you hear from him, okay?"

"Okay. Will you please keep me informed?"

"Yes ma'am, we'll contact you as soon as he's found. In the meantime, try not to worry. I'm sure everything will turn out fine. Thank you for your help. Goodbye now."

Still sobbing. "Goodbye."

He wasn't really sure everything would turn out fine, but he couldn't say that. People who went missing in the thick woods by Half Moon Lake weren't usually okay. He wrote a brief note to the sheriff and left it on his desk. It simply read, "All families contacted, no one has heard from any of them. Frank." He hoped he would be out of the office for the next follow-up call. He was afraid the follow-up would be worse.

Sheriff Mo was in his office having his first cup of coffee. His door was closed, but he could see someone come in through the glass. His phone beeped, and he picked it up.

"Sheriff, there's a Special Agent Bevee here to see you."

He had just posted an APB yesterday. It surprised him that an agent got here so quickly. "Send him in," he said.

Bevee came through his office door, closed it behind him, and said, "Sheriff Broussard, I'm Special Agent in Charge Tyrone Bevee. I'm pleased to meet you."

Sheriff Mo reached out to shake his extended hand as he said, "The ink is barely dry on that missing person report I posted. You guys don't waste any time."

"We try to be efficient, Sheriff. My office stands ready to assist you in your investigation. Would you have a few minutes to bring me up to speed on what you've learned so far?"

"It's still early, and we're not sure what we've got yet, but I'll tell you what I know."

Sheriff Mo explained that the group was renting Roudy's Cabin and that they were given instructions to check in every two days with a satellite phone provided to them. He mentioned Crease delivering supplies and finding no evidence of anything being used two days later. Finally, he told him the families of all the individuals had been contacted and none of the families had heard from them since they went to the cabin.

When he finished with the update, the sheriff asked, "Not to look a gift horse in the mouth, but with what little we know so far, what is it that interests the FBI?"

The position Tyrone Bevee held in the special projects department came with a long list of requirements, both physical and educational. One requirement not on the list, but critically important, was a talent for skillful deception. Something Tyrone Bevee was very good at.

"To begin with, I think you'll have to agree that four grown, healthy men disappearing suddenly is unusual. These men were from New York so that makes it an interstate disappearance. You may not be aware, but at least one individual was of Arab descent, and that opens the possibility of a hate crime. So as you can see, we have several reasons for interest."

"I see. Well, I'm glad to have the help," he said but wasn't sure it was true. There was something about Special Agent in Charge Bevee that rankled him. Something was just a half bubble off plumb.

Agent Bevee asked, "Have you done an extensive

search of the area around the crime scene?"

"No, not yet. It was only yesterday when we had finally spoken to all the families."

"If you'd like, I could conduct that search. I'm sure I have access to more manpower than you do."

"Yes, that would be helpful."

"Consider it done then. I'll let you know what we turn up. Who was the last person to see these gentlemen?"

"They had phone contact with a couple of people while they were still doing their check-ins. The last person to see them physically was Crease Williams. He flew them to the cabin when they arrived."

"I see, and wasn't he the one who took supplies to them a few days ago?"

"That's right."

"He sounds like someone we need to look at closely."

Before construction, workers cleared most trees and shrubs around the site of Roudy's Cabin, leaving only a few mature trees for ascetic reasons. More by accident than design, one area was cleared enough for a helicopter to land. Bevee used this clearing to bring in several loads of national guardsmen to look for the missing campers. Trained search dogs came along with each search team.

Sheriff Mo watched as Bevee directed the search teams, assigning each a specific area to cover. Articles of clothing from the cabin were used to give the search dogs the scent they were to look for. It was difficult to count the number of guardsmen, but Bevee organized a much larger search effort than Sheriff Mo could have put together and for the first time the sheriff was grateful to have the feds' help.

It was still early in the morning when Agent Bevee

sent the search teams out into the thick woods that surrounded the cabin. Each team had a walkie-talkie to keep in contact with the central command post Bevee had set up on the cabin lawn.

"What do you think, Sheriff? Are we going to find anything?" Bevee asked as they watched the search teams disappear into the woods.

Before Bevee had even thought to ask, Sheriff Mo was mulling the possibilities over in his head. He hadn't thought of any scenarios that included the campers found alive and uninjured in the search area around the cabin. If one person was missing, then he could envision him being injured and unable to go for help, sure that could happen. Not four. That made little sense to him. Something bad happened to these guys, not an animal attack, something that involved a human. The sheriff answered him by saying, "I'm not optimistic."

The day passed with each search team checking in over and over but finding nothing. When the sun got low in the sky, Bevee instructed all the teams to come back to the cabin. As they arrived, each team leader would report to Bevee one last time with the news that they had no news. Bevee wrote it all up in a report on his laptop. When he finished, he asked, "What do you think, Sheriff?"

"I don't know what to think. We've never dealt with anything like this before. One missing person, someone who wanders a little too far off the trail...Sure, we get those now and again. Even then we usually find the lost soul in a matter of hours. Four grown men disappearing without a trace, for days? That is something we haven't seen before."

"It happens. I've seen it. Some kind of crime is usually the cause. I think it's time for you to look at this as more than just a missing person case."

Sheriff Mo hated to agree with him, but he was right. Now that they had searched the perimeter of the cabin without finding a clue, it was hard to come up with a scenario where the men got lost or attacked by an animal. With the cabin rental came access to a boat, which was tied up and in good order at the dock. Whatever happened to them, it didn't involve the boat.

Nothing about this made sense to the sheriff. If these four men were involved in something illegal, that might explain it. There was no evidence of that, however. There was no evidence of anything. He was sure lack of evidence wouldn't stop Bevee from making accusations, however. Of that, he was quite sure.

Chapter 6

After the search of the woods around Roudy's Cabin turned up nothing, Agent Bevee was insistent that the sheriff bring in people who had contact with the campers for an interview. Sheriff Mo had no experience investigating what could be a homicide. Bevee knew it and used his lack of experience to manipulate him. He told the sheriff it was standard procedure to "have a chat" with anyone involved. Bevee suggested the logical place to begin was with Crease Williams. Mo knew Crease wasn't involved, so he agreed to call and bring him in for questioning. Crease agreed to come to the sheriff's office first thing in the morning.

Sheriff Mo arrived at his office fifteen minutes before eight. To his surprise, he found Agent Bevee sitting in the waiting area when he walked in the door. "You're startin' kind of early this morning, aren't you, Agent?"

"I like to get an early start to the day when I can."

"Deputy Jensen, what's the coffee situation this

morning?"

"Strong and fresh, just the way you like it, Sheriff," was Jensen's reply.

"Help yourself to a cup if you like, Agent Bevee," Mo said, pointing toward the coffee station.

"Thank you, Sheriff, I think I will."

"Bring your coffee into my office and have a seat."

Bevee did as the sheriff suggested, and Mo did the same. "Crease should be here any time now. What are you going to ask him about?"

Bevee smiled and said, "Just some routine questions. We both agree there's more to this case than simple missing persons. The search around the cabin turned up nothing, and we have to look at other possibilities."

"Maybe so, but Crease has done nothing wrong. I've known him for several years..."

"I've known him longer than you, Sheriff. We attended TCU together."

"You were friends in college?"

"No, not friends exactly. We were teammates in football. I'm afraid I don't share the high opinion you have of him."

"Believe what you want, I've never known Crease to do a dishonest thing since I've known him."

"I'm not saying he's a criminal. We just didn't see eye to eye in college. We were competing for the same position on the team."

"I see, professional rivalry."

"Yes, that's it."

Crease came walking in from outside just then. The sheriff saw him through the glass walls of his office and waved to him to come in. As he came through the office door,

Mo motioned for him to take a seat.

"Thanks for coming in, Crease." He nodded toward his counterpart. "This is Special Agent Bevee. I understand you already know each other?"

Crease looked at Agent Bevee and uncontrollably stared as his mind flipped through the internal Rolodex to confirm what his eyes were seeing. Once he had confirmation it took time for him to try to formulate a response that would relay how he was feeling. He gave up on that and simply said, "Tyrone Bevee. I can't believe it's you."

Bevee, outwardly satisfied at Crease's discomfort, sat back in his chair and relaxed. "Yes, it's been a long time."

While Crease searched for a way to continue, the sheriff said, "Agent Bevee is the FBI's special agent in charge in this district. He's volunteered to help with the missing person investigation."

Crease, finding his wits again, said, "Wow, FBI special agent in charge."

"Don't look so surprised. Did you think I just fell off the edge of the world after graduation?"

"Actually, I never gave it a moment's thought."

Sensing the increase in tension Sheriff Mo said, "We're just doing some routine fact-finding, and we were hoping you could answer some questions about your interaction with the missing campers."

"I'm happy to answer any questions you have, but I'm not sure what I can add to what you already know."

"That's what we're going to find out," Bevee said smugly.

Trying to keep control of the conversation, Mo said, "Let's just get started. This won't take too long."

"Take all the time you need, Mo," Crease said. "I'll help

any way I can."

"I know you will. You aren't suspected of anything."

Bevee, quickly correcting him, said, "Actually, we have yet to eliminate anyone from suspicion."

"I'm going to record this if that's okay," the sheriff said while touching a small tape recorder on his desk.

Crease nodded in agreement.

"All right then, for the record state your formal name, please."

"Tobias Landry Williams."

"You are also known as Crease Williams, is that correct?"

"That's right."

"Conducting this interview, besides myself, is FBI Special Agent in Charge Tyrone Bevee."

"You are a pilot, are you not?"

"I am."

"The Half Moon Wilderness Outfitters employs you to transport people and supplies to remote locations, correct?"

"Yes."

"How often would you say you've done that?"

"I really don't know exactly. I've made dozens of trips ferrying passengers and cargo for the Outfitters."

"Thinking back on the trip when you carried the missing campers to Roudy's Cabin, was there anything unusual or out of the ordinary about it?"

"No. They were excited to begin their vacation, just like anyone else. They were all in good spirits and talked most of the way there."

"Do you remember what they talked about?"

"They were talking among themselves. They did not include me in most of the conversation, but what I recall was typical banter among guys. Things like who would catch the biggest fish or the most fish. How great the weather was going to be. How happy they were to be getting away from work and wives, that sort of thing. Nothing that caused me any concern."

Agent Bevee squirmed in his chair, impatient with the banality of the interview. "Oh, come on, four rich and powerful men spent thirty minutes discussing nothing more interesting than the weather? There were no discussions about money or business dealings?"

Crease, becoming annoyed, said, "I wasn't there to eavesdrop on their conversation. Much of the time I was wearing headphones and could barely hear them at all."

Bevee took over the questioning. "What about the things they packed? Did you see any valuables?"

"No, not that I noticed."

"Did they bring any firearms?"

"There were some rifle cases, but I didn't see what was in them. They brought along a lot of fishing equipment too. They were planning on hunting and fishing, after all."

"What would they have been hunting? What's in season this time of year?"

"I don't know. Ask Mo. I don't hunt. Are we about finished with this?"

"After you dropped them off, what did you do next?"

"I flew back to the Outfitters and docked the floatplane."

"Did you have any contact with them after that day?"

"No, I flew to Texas for the next week."

"Can anyone corroborate that?"

Crease, fully annoyed at the grilling, stood to leave. Bevee sprang up and pointed a finger at his chest. "You don't get to just walk away this time."

"What the hell are you talking about, 'this time?'"

"I mean, you just walked away from football like it was nothing. You took my chance at the big time, then you pissed it away, you lily-white, privileged son of a bitch!"

Crease's response to that accusation was a logical one. He was white. That was hard to argue with, and although he never considered himself privileged, someone who hadn't worked as hard as he did might see it that way. The characterization of his mother as a bitch, however, was why he knocked Bevee on his ass.

"Arrest him!" Bevee shouted from the floor.

"For what?" asked Mo, as if it weren't obvious.

"He assaulted me!"

"You're lucky it was him. If you had said that to me, I'd still be working your ass over."

"Are we done here, Mo?" Crease asked as he headed for the door.

"Yeah, go ahead."

Bevee, about to unravel, said, "Oh, we're not done, not by a long shot!"

Crease ignored him and left the office, fuming.

After Crease stormed out of the office, Mo had to listen to Agent Bevee rant about him for ten more minutes. After Bevee left, Deputy Pride stuck his head in his office door and said, "I only caught the last part of that, but it sounded like one hell of a meeting. Anything I can do to help, boss?"

"If you could tell me where to find those campers, that would be great."

"I can't do that, but the reason I opened your door is that we got the results of the fingerprint search on the criminal database. Here you go." He handed the sheriff a report. "Unfortunately, we didn't get any matches."

"I guess that doesn't surprise me. This case doesn't feel like a typical B and E."

"I agree with you there, boss. It's got me stumped."

"Tell me your take on Special Agent Bevee."

"With all due respect to his position, I don't think his mama held him enough as a baby and he's still pissed off about it."

"Right."

Bevee was a hornet's nest, and Crease had just whacked it with a stick. It was blatantly obvious that Bevee viewed Crease Williams with contempt. Could Bevee investigate objectively? Mo wasn't sure he could, or more accurately, that he had any intention to. At the very least, Mo knew he would take every opportunity to make trouble for Crease, deserved or not.

Crease was the first of a few people the sheriff brought in for some questions. Rose Larson was coming in the afternoon at 1:00 p.m. Then tomorrow he was interviewing a couple of other Half Moon employees who had spoken to the campers when they called to check in and when they ordered supplies.

The sheriff believed these interviews offered as much potential for revealing clues about the disappearance as the interview with Crease did. After seeing his outburst during Crease's interview, and after listening to his unfounded accusations about Crease knowing more than he was telling, Mo would have given odds that Bevee wouldn't show up for the other Q and A sessions.

He wasn't sure if there was anything he could do to rein in the angry Special Agent Bevee. He didn't have any previous experience dealing with feds. He would need to look into that. He did have a plan to help Crease, however, since he was clearly not helping himself.

Special Agent in Charge Tyrone Bevee sat in his high-backed leather executive office chair behind his English oak desk, staring out the window. As he waited for the clock to read nine thirty, he thought about how hard he had worked to get where he was today. The obstacles he had to overcome, the personal sacrifices he had to make, were more substantial than most people would endure. He was proud of what he had achieved in his life.

If he was successful in his current assignment, he could write his own ticket. As exciting as that was, the prospect of being a tool for karma to exact justice on Crease Williams was even more satisfying. He was in a position to have both at the same time. For that to happen, he would have to play his hand carefully, but he believed he held cards good enough to take the whole pot.

Almost exactly as his wall clock registered nine thirty, his phone rang. "Good morning, sir…Thank you, sir…Yes, I oversaw the search personally, in only my designated areas…No sir, nothing…Thank you, sir…Yes, there is one thing, I'm going to need a search warrant, without too many questions asked…Judge Black? Yes, I'll contact him. I think things are going well so far. Yes sir. We'll talk again then. Goodbye."

Who said the government was inefficient? Two minutes on the phone and he had everything he needed. The sheriff was still a potential problem; it was obvious he was another Crease Williams convert, just like in college. For now, he'd let that ride. He saw little the sheriff could do to stop things once they were in motion. If things didn't go well, he could rethink that later.

He would contact Judge Black in a few days after things had settled back down. It would have more of a surprise effect that way. There were times, such as now, when he enjoyed his job so much he was almost glad his football career hadn't worked out. Almost.

Chapter 7

"Where are we going?" Crease asked as he got in the passenger seat of Mo's sheriff's cruiser.

"Just a couple of blocks around the corner. I want to introduce you to a friend of mine."

"A friend of yours? What does he do?"

"What makes you think my friend is a *he*?"

"I've met your wife, and she keeps you on a pretty short leash. I'm betting you don't have any friends who aren't a *he*."

"That's a bet you would lose, my friend. It so happens that I'm taking you to meet my friend Rebecca Larmar. She's about your age and I'm pretty sure not a *he*. She's a local attorney who has a little law office here in town."

"I don't need an attorney, and I'm not looking for a date, so what the hell for?"

"I don't think you appreciate just how much trouble you're in."

"I have done nothing wrong."

"You think that matters? I hear that from just about every criminal I arrest. Do you think that stops me from taking them to jail? No, it doesn't. I'm sure some of them are innocent, but that's not my call. When the DA presents my office with an arrest warrant, it doesn't matter if the subject is guilty or not, or whether I believe he's guilty or not. I can tell you, the ones who have a talented attorney to help them fare a lot better than those who don't."

"You think the DA is going to have me arrested?"

"I'm surprised it hasn't happened already. Look, Crease, just swallow your big Texas pride and ask for some help, okay?"

"Are you always this grouchy in the morning?"

"I'm not grouchy, I'm determined. I'm determined to help you in spite of yourself."

"Okay, lawman, you win. Let's go meet this attorney lady friend of yours."

Sheriff Mo pulled the cruiser up parallel to the curb. The building they were about to walk into was a two-story brick structure, one of the most significant-looking of the offices and small businesses that surrounded the county courthouse and lined the city square. As they entered the glass door, a small directory on the wall showed the law offices of Rebecca Larmar and Associates were on the second floor.

There was no conversation as they started up the staircase. The silence made Crease conscious of the sound of footfalls on the steps. He heard one time that there were always thirteen steps to a gallows. He wondered if that was true, and he wondered how many steps he was climbing now. He didn't count, but he got a queasy feeling as he considered the possibility that Sheriff Mo might be right. Maybe he was in a great deal of trouble.

There was no question in his mind that Bevee hated him and wouldn't miss an opportunity to ruin his life if he could. He wasn't sure if Bevee would allow minor inconveniences like facts to get in his way.

The door to the law office was a nice wooden door with a plate-glass insert, upon which were sandblasted the words Rebecca Larmar and Associates. He wondered if associates meant there were other attorneys or just the receptionist and cleaning lady.

They approached the receptionist's desk a few minutes before nine. The sheriff said they were there to see Ms. Larmer. The receptionist smiled and asked them to have a seat. The reception area was extensive for such a small office. The sheriff chose a seat well away from the desk. From there, they could speak softly and not be heard.

"Why this attorney? Why not someone else?" Crease asked as they sat down.

"Well, for one thing, you may not have noticed, but we aren't exactly overrun with attorneys around here. Even if we were, I'd still bring you here. Beck was what you'd call a child prodigy. She graduated from high school when she was fifteen years old. Then she got a full scholarship to the University of Minnesota, where she got a bachelor's degree in three years. After that, she received a full scholarship to Harvard Law, where she graduated with honors."

"That is impressive. So what is someone that talented doing here in this little town?"

"I could ask the same question about you. What is a potential NFL football star doing here? You have your reasons, and she has hers."

As the large clock above the receptionist's desk pointed straight to nine o'clock, the receptionist picked up the phone and said, "Ms. Larmar, your nine o'clock is here."

They couldn't hear the response on the other end of the phone, but the receptionist hung up and said, "Gentlemen, Ms. Larmar will see you now."

Crease and the sheriff walked toward Rebecca Larmar's office door. The sheriff leaned his head toward Crease and, almost whispering, said, "One thing, life has a way of evening things out, so really smart people aren't usually average looking, you know? So just remember that and try not to stare."

The receptionist opened the office door and motioned them through. Crease walked through first, and before him was an antique oak desk that would have looked at home in a CEO's office. Behind that stood a young lady who he thought was the perfect figure of a female. Five feet and some change tall, with an hourglass figure that would struggle to show triple digits on a bathroom scale. Topped off with wavy auburn hair, emerald-green eyes, high cheekbones, and pearly white teeth shrouded by pouty lips. It was obvious she dressed to appear all business, and the charcoal pinstriped suit she wore tried mightily but failed miserably. Some things are just impossible to disguise.

The young lady behind the desk said, "Hello, gentlemen, I'm Rebecca Larmar."

Crease turned his head and stared at Mo, who just shrugged his shoulders.

Rebecca continued. "I won't ask what that was about. Why don't you gentlemen have a seat and tell me how I might help you."

Crease hoped Mo would take the lead because at that

moment he couldn't remember why they were there.

Thankfully, he did, "Ms. Larmar, I don't know if you remember me. I'm Sheriff Broussard."

"Yes, yes, of course I remember you, Sheriff. Please call me Beck."

"Okay, Beck, my friend here is Toby Williams. I brought him to see you because I'm afraid he's going to need a good attorney soon."

"Okay, Sheriff, let me stop you right there. I'm happy to see if I can help your friend, but in order for the conversation to be protected by the attorney/client shield, it must be a one-on-one exchange."

"Oh sure, I didn't think about that." The sheriff stood up, looked at Crease, and said, "Crease, I've got an errand to run. Explain the situation to Beck, and I'll be back by the time you've finished to pick you up." With that, the sheriff left the office and closed the door.

"Did he call you Crease?"

"Yes, all my friends call me that. It's a nickname I picked up playing football in college. I'd like it if you called me that too."

"All right, Crease, you played football in college?"

"Yes, I did, for TCU. Are you a football fan?"

"No, I'm really not, but that doesn't matter. Tell me why the sheriff thinks you are going to need an attorney."

Crease told her the entire story from the beginning. How he was the one to take the guys to the cabin, to begin with. The fact he delivered supplies to them later and, while there, saw the journal—the journal that disappeared before he took the sheriff to the cabin after the guys were overdue. He explained his relationship with Tyrone Bevee before it all started, including the fact Bevee hates him. Finally, he tells her he took a very effective swing at Bevee during the interview.

When he was finally finished, he asked, "So what do you think?"

Beck sat thoughtfully for a moment and finally said, "The sheriff is right. You're going to need an attorney."

"I don't mean to sound ungrateful, but I was hoping for something more insightful than that. Mo said you are some kind of prodigy."

"I'm smart enough to tell you that being the last person to see these guys before they went missing propels you to the top of the suspect list. How's that for insightful? I'm sorry. I'm guessing the only reason you haven't already been arrested is because of Sheriff Mo. If this Agent Bevee hates you as you say, that won't hold up for long. My advice is to prepare to be arrested. You could be in jail for a long time. Even if you did nothing wrong, if the court doesn't grant your release, either on your own recognizance or on bail, you'll have to stay in jail until they hold a trial, and that could take months."

"You paint a rosy picture, Ms. Larmar."

"Call me Beck. I just want you to be prepared for the worst. I'd be happy to help you if you'd like. Perhaps I can keep you out of jail, at least for now."

"Aren't you going to ask if I had something to do with the disappearance?"

"No, I don't ask defendants if they are guilty. I give them the best defense I can, either way. Besides that, I'm assuming you've convinced Sheriff Mo you had nothing to do with it, and he believes you, so that's good enough for me."

"What do I do now?"

"For now, nothing. If they come to arrest you, call me."

"You can count on it." With that Crease got up and left the office, hoping Mo was back to pick him up.

"You could have warned me," Crease said as he got in the sheriff's cruiser.

"I told you she is a genius before we went in."

"Yes, but you implied she wasn't…that she didn't…"

"I told you not to stare. Did you stare?"

"I don't know, but I'm pretty sure I came off looking like a fool."

"You are overreacting. Besides, she agreed to represent you, didn't she? That's all that matters."

"It's not all that matters."

"Of course it is. You need an attorney and now you've got one. You said you weren't looking for a date."

"Yes, I mean, no, no, I'm not, but still I'd prefer if she didn't think I'm an idiot."

"I'm sure she doesn't."

It was his mom who started the taste of coffee percolating in his mind. He shared many memorable times with his dad, attending Dallas Cowboys games and other sports-related activities. His mom's only sports interest was him. Happy memories with his mom were created on quiet mornings when they chose one of the many local java shops, where they would sample the various coffee-infused drinks while discussing the week's activities or the latest world news. Crease cherished the thought of those times as much as the football memories with his dad.

In the upper-middle-class area of Fort Worth, where they lived, there were no less than six coffee establishments. Sometimes more as they would come and go. Business turnover and ever-changing menu choices meant there were always new concoctions to try. It was a treat he always looked forward to.

The tragic death of his family changed his life in many ways, but one thing that didn't change was his love of coffee. When he moved to this little city of Pine Valley, Minnesota, one of the first things he did was to investigate the coffee venues. It was a task that didn't take long. While coffee was available in every convenience store and diner in town, the sum total of coffee-dedicated enterprises was only one: *Perks Your Interest*.

Despite the feeble name and the general lack of competition, the place had a nice selection of interesting local creations. The building began life as a hardware store, and the coffee shop owners tried to keep as much of the industrial flavor as they could. If it were sitting in a big West Coast city, customers would consider it trendy.

You could find him there most Saturday mornings when he was in town. He waved politely at the other regulars as he walked to the counter and placed his order. He picked from a selection of news magazines and papers before finding a table for two along the back wall.

His week needed a few minutes of quiet contemplation and a good cup of coffee. He had come here often enough to know just about everyone who came in on a Saturday morning. That made it a bit of a surprise when a casually yet sharply dressed young lady came through the door. As far as he could remember, Rebecca Larmar had never been here before, at least not while he was here.

She looked around as if she were scanning the room for something, and it wasn't long before her eyes settled on him. He had many girlfriends in his previous life. No two were alike, but one thing they had in common was they didn't make him nervous. Rebecca Larmar did. She smiled briefly and placed her order. She thanked the clerk, bypassed the selection of news periodicals, and walked slowly, looking for a table. As she approached him, she said, "Hello, Mr. Williams."

"Please, call me Crease. Would you like to sit down?"

"Yes, thank you, I'd like that."

"I don't remember seeing you here before."

"Probably not. I'm not always a coffee drinker."

"So what brings you in today, Rebecca?"

"Not Rebecca. Please just call me Beck."

"I've known a few Rebeccas in my time and many of them went by Becky. I've never known one called Beck. It makes me wonder if that unusual nickname comes with an interesting story."

"There is a story, but I'm not sure about the interesting part. What about you? Crease probably isn't on the top one hundred new baby names." With that, she smiled.

He returned the smile, feeling less nervous now. "Yes, as you said, it comes with a story. Maybe not an interesting one, though."

"Perhaps we should get together sometime and swap nickname stories. I'm afraid I don't have time today."

"I think we should."

"Good, we'll make a plan. The reason I came in here today was that I was told you come here often on Saturday mornings. I was hoping to run into you. Would it be possible for you to take me to the crime scene? I hate to call it that before we know for sure what happened, but that's what the sheriff is calling it."

"Sure, I can fly you there in a floatplane."

"I'm not crazy about flying, but I'm told that is the only way to get there. Is that right?"

"You could take a chopper, but flying is the only way. Why don't you enjoy flying?"

"Mostly the hassle, I suppose. Getting to the airport, shuffling into a plane like a herd of cattle, then being cramped up for two or three hours breathing stale air...It's never been a pleasant experience for me."

"You've never flown in a small plane?"

"No, just big jets. In law school, I flew back and forth a lot."

"I can promise you a ride that will be a lot more fun."

"All right, I'm going to hold you to that."

Chapter 8

As he went through his preflight check and waited for Beck to arrive, he was having difficulty keeping his mind on what he was doing. There was a problem, not with the plane, but in his mind. Just the thought of being around her was enough to bring on the nervous tension. What was that about? It was a new feeling for him, both pleasant and frightening at the same time.

He had dated more than a few ladies in his previous life, in high school and college, before everything changed. None of them made him feel like this. What was different now? He couldn't figure it out. No, that wasn't true. He refused to figure it out or put a name to it. If he did, it would be real, so as long as he didn't name it, maybe it would go away. It had to go away. It was a feeling he couldn't afford, not anymore, not with what he knew.

Just then he looked up and saw her walking toward the plane, smiling brightly. Just the sight of her was all it took for him to realize his mental gymnastics would not work. He couldn't think this feeling away.

As she approached, she gave him a little wave and said, "You look like you're in deep thought."

"Just going through my preflight check. I'd hate to crash and ruin your day," he said lightheartedly.

"I appreciate that."

Boarding a floatplane is really more like climbing into a boat, so he helped her in before climbing in himself. As he pulled away from the dock, he took his time bringing the plane around to position it to take off. He enjoyed giving people the experience of taking off from the surface of a lake.

The thirty minutes it took to fly to the cabin gave them more time to talk casually than they had before. The conversation was about frivolous things. The things people talk about when they are getting to know each other. Neither of them offered insight into the things that made them who they were. He had the feeling those deeper conversations would come sometime later.

As he got out of the plane at the dock, he asked, "Is there something in particular you want to see?"

"No, just take me to the cabin and show me around. If this gets ugly and there's a trial, I like to have seen the location in question."

The thought that there might be a trial wasn't something Crease had really considered before. How could there be a trial when he had nothing to do with the disappearance of the campers? For the moment, he decided not to think about it.

Crease showed Beck around and through the house and finally got to where he had seen and read the now-missing journal. After he had explained about the journal,

Beck asked, "Don't you find it odd that the journal is the only thing disturbed or missing?"

"I can't explain it, but it means someone had to be here after I dropped off the supplies."

"I'll be giving that some thought. I don't like clues I can't explain. I think I'm ready to leave if we've seen the whole place."

As they arrived back at the dock, Beck said, "You were right about the flight. This was the most enjoyable flying experience I've ever had."

"I'm happy to have shared it with you."

He had a restless night. Sleep came easily but was interrupted by dreams that would wake him, even though he couldn't remember them later. All he knew was he awoke smiling and feeling good. That was unusual these last few years. Before last night, the only dreams that woke him were dark, closer to nightmares than dreams.

Yesterday had been more enjoyable than he was expecting, and it took him by surprise. He believed that must have been the source of his broken sleep and pleasant dreams. There was something about Beck, something he noticed the first time they met. He couldn't find a word for it, but it was something different.

He liked the way she made him feel. Not only about the day, but about himself. It was as though he was a better person when he was with her. He remembered his father saying something like that about his mother. He said his mother made him a whole person. He said that was the best way he could think to describe it. He told Crease if he ever found someone who made him feel that way to hang on to them with both arms and not let go. He hadn't really understood that until now.

That was before his life changed. Before his world turned upside down. Not only because of the accident but the other thing as well. There was much more to consider now. A person who made him feel the way his dad felt about his mother would have to be a very special individual. Someone who deserved much more than he had to give. He was nobody's prize, not anymore.

He was going to need her help. Mo was adamant about that, and he trusted Mo's judgment. If there was to be an upcoming fight, she was an ally he needed. He would simply have to keep things on that level. Professional, businesslike, allies in arms. It was at this moment, his moment of quiet determination, that his phone rang.

Somehow he knew, even before he looked at the screen, that it was her calling. The conversation was brief and to the point. She asked if he could meet her for a working lunch. He happily agreed, and she told him to come to her office tomorrow at eleven thirty. She didn't mention what the plan was beyond that, but he didn't care.

That night his sleep was again fleeting and came in brief sessions. Despite that, he woke energized and well-rested. He realized after he had been up for a while that he was watching the clock in anticipation of the lunch date.

As his wristwatch read eleven thirty, he was standing in front of the wall directory that showed the law offices of Rebecca Larson and Associates were on the second floor. Before he went any farther, he heard footfalls on the steps above him. A petite-sounding voice asked, "Crease, is that you?"

"Yes, I'm here. Shall I come up?"

"No, wait there, I'll be right down."

In a few seconds, Beck came down the stairs with a large wicker basket in one hand. Her attire was more casual than he had seen before. He wondered what she had in mind for lunch.

"Are you up for a little walk?" she asked as she reached the bottom of the stairs.

"Sure. Lead the way."

Together, side by side, they walked casually down the street to the corner of the town square and then turned away from it. A couple of blocks later, they came to the city park entrance. Crease had seen the park when he was driving by on the street, but he never had a reason to enter it before. It was obvious she knew it well and knew exactly where she was going.

Soon they were on the bank of a small lake, or large pond, depending on your personal perspective. In the center of the lake was a fountain that sprayed water in all directions. A well-manicured grassy bank surrounded the lake, and there were picnic tables and benches facing the water. On the surface of the lake, white swans and geese swam gracefully.

Beck walked directly to a picnic table as if she had reserved it just for this occasion. She set her basket on one seat of the table and opened the lid. The first item she produced from her basket was a blue-and-white checkered tablecloth, just like you'd see in a lighthearted Hollywood movie. He helped her spread the tablecloth across the top of the picnic table, and she asked, "Shall we sit down?"

"Of course."

Once they were both seated, she opened the lid of the wicker basket again and said, "I hope you like fried chicken." He smiled and nodded in approval, and much to his surprise, what she brought out of the basket wasn't in a commercial fast-food container. Instead, she produced a foil-covered china plate. Even though the pan-fried fowl wasn't piping hot, it smelled wonderful. It prompted him to ask, "Do you like to cook?"

"Some things, yes. I'm not an accomplished chef, but my grandma taught me how to prepare a few things. I hope it's to your liking."

He was hungry, and he didn't get home cooking these days, so after she had provided plates and napkins, he was ready to dig in.

She said, "Fried chicken is best enjoyed with your fingers."

He couldn't agree more. The taste took him back to Sunday dinners with his mom and dad. He hadn't had chicken that tasted like this in many years. He asked Beck, "You made this yourself?"

"Yes, do you like it?"

"It tastes just like what my mother used to make."

"I'll take that as a compliment," she said with a smile. "I also made some potato salad," she said, handing him a container.

He dipped out a portion, and for the next few minutes, they sat, eating without conversation. It was unusual for him to sit, one on one with someone, and not feel compelled to say something. He realized just how comfortable he had gotten with Beck since their first meeting.

After he had discarded his last chicken bone, Beck reached into her basket and pulled out a roll of moistened wipes. It seemed she had thought of everything. He cleaned his face and wiped his fingers with a towelette. His stomach was telling him he had eaten too much, but it was too good to stop.

When he saw she had finished eating as well, he opened a conversation. "Fill in some blanks for me. You are a highly educated attorney, schooled at some of the best institutions in the country. You could have a corner office in a high-rise office building in New York, a partner in a big, successful law firm. Why do you choose to live here?"

"It's a bit of a long story."

"I've got time if you do."

"Okay then. When I was a child, my mother realized early on that I was quick to learn things. My teachers confirmed that during parent-teacher conferences. She went to the school board and petitioned them to create a program for gifted kids. She had to take on a lot of the responsibilities herself to get it created. I was one of a few students who were the first of a long list of gifted students who would come later."

"It was her efforts that allowed me to graduate from high school early, and to get scholarships to attend the University of Minnesota. Whatever the scholarships didn't pay for, my parents picked up. When I finished my undergraduate degree, I didn't even have student loans to pay back."

Crease said, "It sounds like you have amazing parents."

"Yes, they are. When I continued my education with Harvard Law, they were having some serious problems and couldn't support me as much. I had to take out several student loans to finish my law degree. After that, I could see how much trouble they were having with daily life. I wanted to help them as much as possible. I opened my little law office here and I visit them regularly to help them."

When he realized she had finished her story, he said, "That speaks well of you. Many people wouldn't do what you are doing. So where did 'Beck' come from?"

"My grandpa had a stroke just about the time I was born. He lost the use of his legs and one of his arms. He also had speech difficulties. He could form one-syllable words pretty well but had trouble putting words together. I was his first grandchild, and as hard as he tried, he could only say 'Beck.' That caught on with the rest of the family and I've been Beck ever since."

"That story is both tragic and sweet at the same time. Is your grandpa still around?"

Beck, looking down at the table, said, "No, he passed away when I was seventeen."

"I'm sorry to hear that. How are your parents getting along?"

"They really struggle some days, but other days are okay. They just never know."

"What caused their health problems?"

"My dad served in the Gulf War. He spent some time in a field hospital. My mom was a nurse who cared for him. They fell in love and got married after the war. They both suffer from what is called Gulf War syndrome. There's a lot of debate and many theories about what causes it, but they both have intermittent cognitive issues. I go by their house and make sure they have everything they need."

"Family is very important to you, isn't it?"

"Yes, very much so. If you don't have family, what have you got?"

Crease simply smiled in response.

"Oh no, I'm so sorry. I just didn't think."

Crease tried to ease her conscience with his expression

and said, "Don't worry about it. I agree with you, family is everything, except maybe for health. With both family and health, you just don't realize what you have until you lose it."

"Your mom and dad were all you had, weren't they? You don't have any siblings?"

"No, I was an only child. It's funny when I say that now it sounds unusual, but growing up, I never gave it a thought. I never asked my parents if there was a reason I was their only child. Now I wish I had."

"Wow, this little lunch meeting took a dark turn in a hurry."

"Yeah, maybe that's because you and I both have seen our share of life's dark side."

There was a silence for a while until finally Beck perked up and said, "Maybe this is a turning point. I'm not a believer in predestination, but I'm saying the fact that we met at this point in our lives will be the beginning of something better."

Crease was both excited and frightened to hear what she was saying. He wasn't sure how to respond, but it turned out he didn't have to. Beck continued.

"Throughout school I was always younger than the other students in the room. If I wanted to be noticed, I had to speak my mind. It became a habit that I still have, so I'm going to speak my mind here too. I enjoy spending time with you. When I asked you to do this working lunch, that was a bit of a ruse. I just wanted to see you again. There is something about you. When I'm with you I feel like I'm a more complete person. Do you understand what I'm saying?"

At first Crease was too dumbfounded to reply. Listening to Beck, Crease thought it sounded like he was hearing an echo of the thoughts in his mind. It made him both happy and sad at the same time. Happy to know that he wasn't alone in the way he was feeling. Sad because he knew he could never allow a relationship to grow. Not with what he knew. He was also sad to think he might have to share what he knew with someone for the first time, so she would understand why there could be no relationship, no future for them.

For now, however, he could at least tell her he understood. There was no harm in that, so he said, "Yes, I understand what you are saying. I have had those same thoughts myself lately." After saying that, he reached out with his hand, and she took it.

Chapter 9

Sheriff Mo came into the office early. He hadn't slept well. He didn't see the point of lying in bed wondering why he hadn't heard from Agent Bevee. So he came into the office and wondered instead. It had been a few days since the interview with Crease and Bevee, and given how it ended, he couldn't believe Bevee would allow things to lie quietly for very long. He didn't enjoy waiting to see what Bevee's next move would be. He didn't have to wait much longer.

Mo and Deputy Pride were discussing the failures of the Vikings' coaching staff in the previous NFL game when the front door opened and Agent Bevee stormed into the outer office. Behind him were two fellow agents. Without invitation, Bevee marched into Mo's office. "I have a search warrant for the residence of Crease Williams to be served immediately." As he made this declaration, he slapped the warrant papers down on Mo's desk.

The sheriff picked up the papers and read them briefly.

"They appear to be in order, but what the hell are you looking for?"

"Anything connected to the disappearance of the individuals who went missing from Roudy's Cabin. We are ready to proceed at once."

Bevee's arrogance annoyed the sheriff, but he tried not to show it. Leaning back in his chair he said, "You may be ready, but this is news to me. I've got an appointment to meet with the city council this morning. It will be a couple of hours before I'm free to serve your warrant."

"I'll take one of your deputies then. There's no reason to wait. We can handle the search."

"My deputies don't work for you. Neither do I. Come back in two hours, after the city council meeting, and we'll go execute your warrant."

Frustrated, Bevee said, "You do understand notice of the warrant is not allowed, correct?"

"I know my job, Bevee. I don't need you to explain it to me."

Bevee picked up the warrant papers and headed for the door. As he was about to exit he turned and said, "We'll be back in two hours. Be ready." He and his fellow agents exited the office.

After the agents were gone, Deputy Pride looked at the sheriff and said, "I thought the city council meeting was next week."

"I think you may be right. My mistake." The sheriff took a sip of coffee and sat thoughtfully for a moment. "We're going to need another deputy."

"You think there will be trouble?"

"I think Agent Bevee *is* trouble, and I don't want to go outnumbered."

"Frank just came off the overnight shift. He's going to need some sleep about now."

"Call the Bobcat Grill. Ask for Frances Hannigan's number."

"Are you going to deputize Tiny Hannigan again?"

"When you get his number, call and tell him if he can be here in an hour, it'll go a long way toward resolving that little traffic infraction he had last month."

Laughing, Deputy Pride said, "Yes sir."

Tiny Hannigan worked at the Bobcat Bar and Grill. When the Bobcat opened its doors, the owner wanted it to be a place where people could go for a night of fun. They served good food, nothing fancy, but satisfying. On Friday and Saturday nights, there was live music provided by local talents. An ample dance floor invited people to shake and shimmy their problems away, if only for an evening.

At first, the Bobcat was, as intended, a friendly, enjoyable place to be. However, as with most things in life, things don't always go as planned.

After it had been open for a few weeks, the Bobcat became known for having good food and lively music. The crowds on the weekends grew, and with the growth came an element of society whose idea of a good time included starting trouble and picking fights at the drop of a hat. For a while, calls to the sheriff's office on Saturday night became a regular occurrence and business suffered.

Then, a little over two years ago word around town was that the Bobcat had hired a new doorman. Even in a small town like Pine Valley, where everything anyone did was news, a new doorman was of little interest to Sheriff Mo except the doorman's name was Frances. In a venue where some people looked for a reason to start trouble, a doorman named Frances might as well have a "hit me" sign on his back. The sheriff looked for trouble at the Bobcat to become even more of a problem.

The first Saturday night after the Bobcat hired Frances Hannigan, a call came in as usual. There were three unruly types who were asking young ladies to dance and then fighting with their husbands or boyfriends when they objected. Mo gathered a couple of deputies and headed for the bar, figuring they would have to break up a fight like they had done many times before. Instead, and much to his surprise, they walked in the door and found Frances, who he later learned preferred to be called Tiny, with the situation well in hand.

There was Tiny Hannigan standing with one troublemaker's head locked under each arm. The third was lying on the floor with Tiny's foot firmly planted on his neck. All three looked like they'd had a ton of bricks fall on them. Tiny politely asked Sheriff Mo what he wanted to do with them. He told Tiny they would take it from here. The three losers seemed genuinely happy to be taken into custody.

Frances had been raised by his mother alone. He tipped the scale at eleven pounds when he was born and was always a head taller than the other kids in his class. His father was an alcoholic who left home before Frances was five years old. He would show up when he needed money and take everything his mother had. That was until Frances turned seventeen years old. The last time his father showed up for money, Frances told him to leave. Instead, his father, drunk, told Frances he was going to teach him a lesson. Frances beat him within an inch of his life. He never came back again.

Calls from the Bobcat became less frequent after that first night until after a couple of months, there were no calls at all. Since then, the sheriff had deputized Tiny on a couple of occasions when he was a little shorthanded, or if he really wanted to get someone's attention.

Agent Bevee was prompt. He came through the door precisely two hours after he left the office. He came into the sheriff's inner office and asked, "Are we ready to proceed?"

"Yes, you follow us," was the sheriff's reply.

Sheriff Mo, Deputy Pride, and newly deputized Tiny Hannigan climbed into the sheriff's SUV and headed to Crease's house. Agent Bevee and company were in another car, following closely behind. Mo drove slowly. He dreaded presenting Crease with a search warrant. He knew Crease had nothing to hide, and the warrant was nothing but a harassment ploy by Agent Bevee.

They pulled up in front of the little house that Crease called home these days. Mo took the key out of the ignition and sat for a second, trying to think of a way to avoid what he was about to do. Nothing came to him. To nobody in particular, he said, "Let's get this over with."

By the time he got the car door open, Agent Bevee was already standing on the street, looking at him. Sheriff Broussard, Deputy Pride, and Deputy Hannigan all climbed out of the SUV. As a group, they walked up the narrow sidewalk to the front door of a small bungalow with white vinyl siding. The house was probably eighty years old but didn't look it. The siding was clean and the roof was new. The front door was hunter green, steel clad with an oval etched-glass window.

As he led his deputies to the door, it occurred to him he had never been to Crease's home before. He looked around for a doorbell, but finding none, he knocked. He could hear footfalls inside the house coming closer to the door. This was the moment he'd been dreading since Agent Bevee burst into his office this morning.

Crease opened the door, obviously surprised at the caravan of law enforcement standing on his porch. He said, "Sheriff, what's all this?"

"I'm sorry about this, Crease, but there's been a warrant issued to search your home." Bevee stepped forward and stuck out his hand with the warrant. Crease didn't take it and was at a loss for words.

Bevee didn't wait for words to come to him. He said, "Please step aside."

Crease just looked at him defiantly. Finally, Sheriff Mo said, "Come on, Crease, don't make this any harder than it has to be. Let him do his search and we'll be out of here."

Crease slowly, reluctantly moved aside just far enough for the agents to pass. Bevee didn't waste any time. He led the agents into the room, where he directed each of them to search in a separate room. Bevee himself started in the living room, where they were standing.

Bevee started opening drawers and digging through the contents. He moved from one piece of furniture to another, leaving no drawer unopened. Sounds emanating from the other rooms said the other agents were doing the same thing.

Crease had held his tongue as long as he could and told Mo, "Sheriff, this is bullshit."

"I know, but there's nothing I can do about it. Just hang in there a little longer." As he said this the noise coming from the other rooms stopped. There was silence briefly until an agent came into the room and called to Agent Bevee. The agent held some items in his hand and was showing them to Special Agent Bevee. They talked among themselves for a moment until Bevee took the items and brought them over where Crease and Sheriff Mo were standing.

Bevee held one hand out to the sheriff and said, "I believe the names on the IDs in these two wallets match two of the missing campers, don't they, Sheriff?"

Mo was shocked but looked at the two leather wallets Bevee was holding. By now, Mo had the names of the campers committed to memory, so it didn't take him long to say, "Yes, they do."

Bevee continued. "And this journal certainly fits the description of the journal Mr. Williams claimed to have seen on his supply run, does it not?"

The sheriff took the journal and looked through the pages. Crease strained to look over his shoulder. Mo looked at Crease and raised the journal as if to ask, *Is this it*?

Crease answered aloud, "That looks like the same journal, but the last entry is missing. None of those things were here. You planted that stuff!"

Bevee smiled a very self-aggrandizing smile. "Sheriff, I think you know what you must do now."

Sheriff Mo looked at the items the agent found for a moment and said, "I'm not sure what you are trying to say, Bevee."

"You've got to arrest him!" The three agents crowded closer, trying to intimidate the sheriff. Deputy Pride realized what was happening and nudged Tiny. They both stood up close to Sheriff Mo. With Tiny in attendance, the federal agents no longer appeared intimidating.

"I'm going to need more investigation before I arrest anyone, and like I've said before, Bevee, I don't work for you."

Bevee was livid. Before he stomped out of the house, he told the sheriff, "Suit yourself if that makes you feel better. I'll be bringing a report of the search to the district attorney. There's going to be an arrest, mark my words, Sheriff." Bevee took the items and quickly left the premises, his fellow agents in tow.

After they left, Crease turned to the sheriff, "I don't know where those items came from."

"I believe you, son, but I don't think that matters much. Bevee will be true to his word. He'll push the DA for an arrest warrant."

"That journal, it no longer had the page I read that day in the cabin. The entry that read they had found something interesting they wanted to go back and explore."

"With the journal found, and you agreeing it's the one you saw, they can claim you made up the entry you say you read."

"But why?"

"I'm not sure. It's like they don't want anyone to believe the campers found something, but why would Bevee care about that? I'm going to give it some thought."

"What should I do?"

"You do nothing. I mean it. You lie low for a while. Don't fly back to the cabin or the surrounding woods. In fact, stay away from Half Moon altogether, got it? I'm probably going to be forced to arrest you, and if you go back to the cabin area, it is going to be seen as you trying to hide something, so just stay home until you hear from me."

"That will not be easy for me, Mo. I don't enjoy being persecuted."

"I know, but just let me handle it for a while. Call Beck, tell her I said you are likely to be arrested so she'll be ready."

"I'm not sure how I'll deal with jail."

"I know, and I'm telling you to prepare Beck for the

possibility so she can get you out as soon as possible. While you're there, we'll make sure you get a cell with some really friendly types." Mo smiled as he said that.

"Thanks a lot, Sheriff."

During the drive back to his office, Mo's mind was racing. He thought he would feel better to have the search behind him. It would just be a temporary inconvenience for Crease, one he would hate, and one Mo hated to put him through. No question about either of those things, but then it would be over, and that would be the end of it.

That wasn't the end of it, the way it worked out. Instead of feeling relieved to have it over and done, Mo was wondering what to think about evidence being found. He didn't even like using that word, "evidence." It made it sound as though Crease had done something illegal, and he couldn't believe that. Still, it definitely wasn't over, no matter what he believed.

He thought about it logically. What would a person gain by taking the items that were found? The two wallets for cash and maybe credit cards? Mo didn't know Crease's financial situation, but he always had the impression money wasn't an issue. Was he wrong about that? He didn't think so, but he could confirm that.

What about the journal? He'd already mentioned his thoughts about the journal to Crease. If they wanted people to believe Crease made up the last entry, why? To destroy his credibility? Maybe, but the same question remains, why? This would require a lot more thought.

Crease stood at the front door and watched Sheriff Mo, Deputy Pride, and Deputy Hannigan drive away. He didn't know it, but he and the sheriff were having the same thoughts. Except Crease had a little more knowledge to work with. He knew he hadn't stolen those items. He had to believe Bevee had planted them. So why plant the journal, but remove the last entry? To make it look like he was losing his mind? To make it appear as though he wasn't to be believed? Either, or both, of those thoughts could be true. He sure felt like he was losing his mind.

Had he really read an entry about finding something interesting? He even doubted himself, but he did. He remembered it. It wasn't important, just a scrawl in a diary that seemed to explain where the campers were and why they didn't meet him at the dock that day. It was no big deal, not then. Now it was, and he wished he had copied it down. He couldn't remember what it said word for word, but something about hiking and finding something, but what? He remembered enough to know it didn't say, so why would Bevee hide it? He must have. Who else could it be? His head was spinning.

He had to stop attempting to make sense of it all alone. He needed a sympathetic ear. Someone who would not only listen with interest but also bring intelligent ideas to the discussion. He had the perfect person in mind. Mo said he needed to call her anyway. So he did.

Beck suggested under the circumstances, it might be good to hold their discussion while having a bit of fun. The Bobcat Bar and Grill had live music for the evening, so Beck had her assistant book a table. Crease was happy to have a night out with Beck. It would be good to think about something other than the search of his home, not to mention the prospect of being arrested.

At the same time, however, his ever-present defense mechanism was urging caution. It was as though he had an unseen chaperone staring him down at the mere possibility of a faux pas. He was growing to hate it. For the last ten years, it had prevented him from allowing anyone to get too close. That had been okay with him. He understood why deep relationships weren't possible, not for him.

Now, this time, it was different. For the first time, he saw the defense mechanism as a foe, not a friend. He wanted to yell at it as if it were a real person. *Leave me the hell alone! I know the consequences. Just allow me to enjoy the moment.* He decided to do just that, enjoy the moment. There would be plenty of time to consider consequences later.

The day seemed to pass slowly. They were to meet at eight o'clock, but eventually it was time. He pulled the car into the parking lot beside the Bobcat Grill and found a space without too much trouble. It looked to be a full, but not packed, crowd. He walked in the door and was about to tell the hostess he had a reservation when he saw Beck waving to him from across the room.

He walked to the table where Beck was sitting, and as he sat down, he saw she was beaming. Just the sight of her smiling so enthusiastically was enough to lift his spirits. The light was dim around the dance floor where Beck was sitting and his eyes hadn't adjusted yet, but even so, he said, "You look nice this evening." Because he knew it was true. She responded with, "Why, thank you, sir."

He sat down at the table, and a server came to get their drink order. Beck ordered a glass of white wine and Crease said he'd have a Pearl. Beck wondered what a Pearl was, but she didn't ask. It wasn't until the server brought the drinks that she realized Pearl was a beer. Curiosity got the better of her and she said, "I don't think I've ever seen Pearl beer before."

"Probably not if you have spent no time in Texas. The only Pearl brewery is in Fort Worth these days. When I was growing up, Pearl was the only beer my dad ever had in the house. When I fly back to Texas, I bring back a few cases with me. The owner here at the Bobcat keeps some on hand for me."

"That's interesting. So even though you've been here for years, you're still a Texas boy at heart?"

"Something like that. It's hard to explain to people who aren't from Texas. I don't believe everything is better in Texas, or bigger, or that life ends when you leave Texas. Yet, I always consider myself a Texan, no matter how many years I've been away. There's a comfort and pride that I get from being born in Texas."

"I don't feel any special pride tied to my birthplace, so I find your feeling to be rather odd but interesting."

Just then, the server appeared and asked if they needed anything and that thankfully changed the subject.

Beck said, "Tell me about today. You received a brief visit?"

"Yes, Bevee and two other agents showed up with Mo and presented me with a search warrant. I know it wasn't Mo who was responsible. I'm not angry with him."

"What did they claim to find?"

"One agent came out of the bedroom claiming to have found two wallets that belong to the campers, and also the journal I saw the day I dropped off supplies."

"I don't normally ask my clients if they are guilty, but..."

Crease broke in and said, "No, I didn't take those things. I had never seen the wallets before, but I had seen the journal. I read the last passage in it the day I was there, but that entry was missing when they presented it today."

"That's interesting. Why would they remove the last

entry? Why would they pretend to find it in your house?"

"I don't know, I've been thinking about it, but I just don't know."

"Do you remember who signed the search warrant?"

"I don't know what you mean."

"A judge must approve a search warrant. It would have been at the bottom of the paper they gave you when they came into your house."

"Oh, okay. Yes, I remember seeing it. It was…Black, that was it, Judge Black."

"All right, I'll look into who Judge Black is. I'm surprised they didn't arrest you today."

"Bevee wanted it, but Mo wouldn't do it."

"I don't think he'll be able to hold them off too long. You need to be prepared to be arrested."

"Okay, what does that mean? I'm afraid I have no experience with being arrested."

"They will come and take you down to the sheriff's office. You'll be photographed, fingerprinted, and interviewed. Then they will put you in jail."

"Sounds like a party so far. How long will they keep me?"

"It depends. You'll be brought before a judge, where the charges against you will be read. He will either release you with a promise that you'll return for trial, or you'll have to put up a bail amount to be released. Bail money is used to track you down if you run away, and the amount depends on a lot of things. It could be as much as one hundred thousand dollars. What most people do is get a bail bondsman to supply the bail money, and for that, they charge ten percent. Can you come up with ten thousand dollars to pay a bondsman?"

"Let me make sure I understand this. I can pay ten thousand bucks to a bondsman for him to put up the whole one hundred thousand, and when I show up for court, he gets his one hundred back and he keeps my ten, right?"

"Yes, that's how it works."

"I'm not paying anybody for basically doing nothing. I know I'll show up for court, so I'll just put up the one hundred thousand myself."

Beck took a few seconds to process what he had said. "So you've got that kind of money to post on your own?"

Crease sighed and fumbled with the saltshaker. "Yeah, money isn't a problem for me. My dad prepared for the unexpected quite well."

"Well, okay then, that makes things easier. I will try to keep bail from being excessive, but you never know. Good to know we have a backup plan."

The band started playing a song that was bringing several couples out on the floor. Crease stood, reached out his hand, and said, "How about we stop talking about money and dance awhile?" Beck smiled and took his hand.

They danced the evening away. They talked about legal issues now and again, but mostly they danced. By the end of the night, Crease knew he had a real problem, and it had nothing to do with Agent Bevee.

He stood by his desk, looking out the window. Agent Bevee didn't mind receiving these regular calls from the assistant director. Updating him on the progress he was making was a part of the job. He was standing because what he was about to report frustrated him. He wished he could report everything was going precisely as planned, but he could not.

The sheriff was even more of a problem than he originally thought. The man was too stubborn for his own good. He was just a simple county sheriff. What was going on was way over his head. He should stop standing in the way of progress.

He glanced at his watch; it read nine thirty on the nose. Before he could get his sleeve pushed back into place, the phone rang. You could find fault with the AD in some ways, but he was prompt.

"Good morning, sir…Yes, I've made progress. I used the search warrant to gain access to the subject's home, and I presented the evidence to the local sheriff…Yes sir. I wish I could say so, but the sheriff refused to make the arrest… Thank you, sir, I think that would be helpful. I appreciate any assistance dealing with this county official. Yes sir…I'm not sure I trust the local DA to do what he's told…Yes sir, that's what I was thinking…Yes sir…I'm happy to do it…Thank you, sir. Goodbye."

Chapter 10

Once again Crease had a restless night. Sleeplessness was becoming a regular thing. Between the search of his house, and the specter of arrest hanging over his head, he wasn't able to shut his mind down at night. Last night was even worse, but at least it was for a good reason. He and Beck had danced until the Bobcat Grill was ready to close. It was the most enjoyable evening he had in a long time.

As he lay quietly in bed this morning, it was not Beck that filled his mind. He kept thinking about the journal, what he had read in it, and why it showed up in his house. It said they found something interesting. What did they find? Was it something valuable? Could it have been something illegal? He entertained that last thought briefly. He had heard about cannabis patches in the woods before. That was farther south, though. He didn't think marijuana would grow in this cold climate. No, that couldn't be it.

He needed to do more than think about it. He needed to

go search around. He wasn't there when the first search was conducted. At the time he didn't see any reason to be there. Now, however, with Bevee planting evidence in his house, he questioned how thorough a Bevee-led search might have been. He would not go hiking through the brush. That would be too time consuming for one person. He could search from the air instead.

Sheriff Mo had told him not to leave the area or fly, but he wasn't really going anywhere. He would land back at the same place he took off. It was more of a joyride. He figured that would be okay, but of course he didn't plan to ask. He had to do it, even if he stood little chance of finding anything. It would make him feel better.

He got out of bed, showered, dressed, and nuked a couple of tamales. He packed a pair of binoculars and a small camera in case he got lucky. His Cessna needed fuel and for that, he would have to go into the office and talk to Rose. Any other time he would enjoy that, but he figured Rose had heard about everything by now, including the fact the sheriff grounded him. He was going to catch hell from Rose.

Crease walked into the radio room of the Outfitters, smiling as if he didn't have a care in the world. Rose turned to see him immediately and said, "Crease Williams, I sure wasn't expecting to see you soon. Not with all you have going on. I'll bet you just missed seeing me, is that it?"

"I miss you the minute I walk out the door."

"Come over here and give me a hug, you big sexy linebacker."

Letting "linebacker" pass without notice, he did as she asked. "How have you been lately, Rose?"

"I'm still here for the taking, darlin'. How about you? I

hear the feds came and paid you a little visit."

"I figured you had heard about that. I'm all right. Mad as hell about it, but I'm all right."

"Hang in there, darlin', you'll get through this. People who know you don't believe you did anything wrong. So what brings you out here besides getting a hug from me?"

"I thought maybe a little joy ride in my Cessna would calm my nerves. I'm low on fuel and I came in to get the key to the pump."

"Joy ride? Darlin', do you take me to be much younger and more naive? You don't want any joy ride. You want to fly up around Roudy's Cabin to find something."

"Well, damn it, Rose, what if I do? They put my butt in a sling and I'd like to remove it."

"Sheriff Mo grounded you."

"No, not officially."

"Officially or not, he agreed not to arrest you with the understanding you wouldn't go anywhere."

"I'm not going anywhere. I'm gonna go up, fly around, and come right back here. No one will even know I left. Come on, Rose, help me out here."

"Don't go flashing that toothy grin at me. Okay, I'll give you the key on one condition. I'm going with you."

"Now wait a minute, Rose—"

"No, that's the deal. I've never been up in one of those planes before, and besides that, if you don't come back I'm gonna tell them you kidnapped me. Do we have a deal?"

"All right, Rose, you win. Get the key and let's go."

They went down to the airfield and Crease filled the plane with fuel. He helped Rose get into her seat and went around and got in himself. As he was preparing to start the engine, Rose asked, "So where are we going?"

"I'm not sure exactly."

"Well, what are we looking for?"

"I don't know."

"Then how will you know if we find it?"

"I'm not sure I will."

"It seems to me this operation is missing some important details."

"Look, Rose, the journal I read said something about finding something interesting. Whatever it was interested them enough to go back the next day, and no one has seen them since. I don't think we're looking for a rare butterfly. We'll just look for something that doesn't belong. That's really all I have to go on."

"Okay, darlin', that works for me."

They took off and Crease pointed the plane toward Roudy's Cabin. He figured starting there and flying in an ever-enlarging circular pattern made as much sense as anything. He told Rose to take the bag with the binoculars and camera and use them when she needed to.

When they were in sight of the cabin, he got a sick feeling in his gut. That was sad. He used to enjoy flying to the cabin and pulling up to the dock. Now there was no joy in it at all. He dropped to a fairly low altitude. He really wasn't sure what altitude gave him the best chance of seeing something. Especially since he didn't know what they needed to see.

Round and round they went with Crease looking forward and to the left as much as possible, while Rose had her nose stuck to the right-side window. Occasionally Rose would put the binoculars up to her eyes and peer through them briefly. Then she'd lower them again.

They had been in the air for almost an hour since they

left the cabin area. He didn't know how far away they were as the crow flies, but he figured this was about as far as the campers could have hiked and still gotten back to the cabin in the daylight of one day. He decided he would make one more circle and call it a day.

Suddenly Rose jerked the binoculars up to her face and exclaimed, "What's that?"

"What? I see nothing."

"I don't know, but I saw something. Just a quick glimpse and then it was gone."

"What did it look like?"

"Nothing exactly. It wasn't trees or brush. I saw straight lines and maybe some turned ground. Can you go back around?"

Crease tried to get the plane turned in the opposite direction while not losing his bearings. He wanted to take a longer approach to the area and pass it on the left, so Rose might see it again. He came around and straightened out his heading. He realized he was holding his breath, hoping Rose saw something, anything, important.

"I think we are coming up on the area again. Keep your eyes peeled."

Seconds passed, and with each one, his hopes fell. Then Rose yelled, "There it is! Damn, it's gone already."

"Did you see more this time? Can you tell what it is?"

"All I can say is it's a structure. I can't tell much more than that, but it's definitely man-made."

"Okay, look at this gauge and write those coordinates. At least we'll be able to find it again."

Rose quickly copied the readings. As she finished, it happened again. The engine, gauges, everything went blank and silent. The plane took a sharp lurch downward as Rose cried, "Holy shit, Crease, what did you do? Are we going to crash?"

Crease struggled with the yoke, trying to keep the altitude up. Then, as quickly as it stopped, everything came on again. Rose was in the middle of a prayer as it did. "Darlin', please get us home and I promise never to ask to fly with you again."

He didn't waste any time getting the plane headed back toward Half Moon Field. Once his heart stopped pounding, he smiled. They had found something. There shouldn't be any structures this far north in the woods. As a bonus, the plane cut out while Ol' Pete's device was engaged, and they didn't crash. Maybe Pete could figure out what's wrong with it. A pretty good day.

Little did he know, while he was feeling good about things, eyes were watching.

Chapter 11

When they landed, Rose couldn't wait to get her seat belt off and get out of the Cessna. As she was walking up to the Outfitters, she said, "I'll never climb in one of those damned things again. I could have died today. As it is, I think I got scared out of ten years of life."

"Sorry, Rose," Crease called to her as she walked away.

"You are lucky to be good-lookin' or I'd tie your ears in a knot. Scarin' an old woman like that. You should have told me that plane had a problem."

He wouldn't tell her, but he was just as scared as she was. He had simply been through it before. He sure hoped Pete could find the problem. It's not much use having a nice plane that you were afraid to fly.

His chief concern was figuring out what Rose saw in the timber, but while he was here and Ol' Pete was just up the hill, he'd stop in and tell him he should have some data to analyze.

When he got to the building, he hoped Rose hadn't gotten back to her desk yet, and he was in luck. He walked on through the warehouse, back to the maintenance area where Pete could usually be found. Sure enough, there he was behind his desk with his feet propped up on it, smoking one of those gas station cigars.

"Hey, Pete, Rose and I just took my Cessna up for a little spin, and it cut out again. Just like it did the first time."

Ol' Pete took a drag from his cigar, then took it out of his mouth. "I thought Sheriff Mo grounded you."

"Well, no, not officially. Geez, you sound like Rose. I had your device activated while I was flying, so if it works like you say it will, you can figure out what the problem is, right?"

"It'll work. I didn't spend all that time creating something that won't work. Leave me the key and I'll look at it when I'm not so busy."

Crease couldn't think of a polite answer to that, so he just left. He knew Pete would look at the plane. Not so much because he cared about the plane problems. He would just want to see if his device worked.

In the meantime, Crease had to figure out what to do about the structure Rose saw. She didn't see enough to know what it was, but he had to believe it was what the campers were interested in. There just wasn't much else to see up there.

He would tell Mo about it, but since Mo told him not to fly, he didn't know how to bring it up. He had to figure something out. Things were unraveling, and that building, or whatever it was, had to be a part of it.

***

Special Agent in Charge Tyrone Bevee was in his office working on a report about the current situation in Pine Valley. His phone rang and when he picked it up, it surprised him to find the call was from the lab. They rarely called him in the office. He was there often enough, so there was no reason to. Unless they had bad news.

"Hello?"

"Agent Bevee, this is Agent Rawlings. I wanted to let you know we've had another security breach."

"What now?"

"Well, sir, we had a plane fly over. It wasn't just a flyby. They circled around and came back over the top of the lab."

"What kind of plane? Was it military?"

"No sir, it was a single-engine civilian plane, a Cessna, I believe. One agent got the tail number. We checked the registration. It belongs to Toby Williams."

"Why does that not surprise me? Our scapegoat is becoming a real pain in the ass. He will not let this go. One way or the other, I'm going to remove him from the equation. Increase security around the perimeter. Call me if there are any other visitors."

"Yes sir, I will keep you informed."

Mo walked across the sidewalk to the office door with a feeling this might not be the best day. Then he stopped himself. With his hand on the door, he decided he was just borrowing trouble. He shouldn't worry about things until they happen. His mood improved a little.

He opened the door and walked across the room to his office. He hung up his jacket and looked for his coffee cup. He found it. He picked it up and turned to head for the coffee station. Standing in his office doorway was Deputy Jensen.

Seeing Jensen, standing with a somber look on his face, the sheriff gritted his teeth and said, "Frank, before you say anything, I want you to ask yourself two questions. First, do I like my job? Second, is what I'm about to tell the sheriff going to make him mad enough to fire somebody?"

"Ah, well, yeah, I like my job—"

Mo cut him off. "Out with it, Frank. What's so urgent it can't wait until I've had my coffee?"

"Well, Sheriff, it's just that I took a message a few minutes before you walked in. The district attorney wants you to come to his office as soon as possible."

"Can't I just call him?"

"No sir, he said it was important you come to see him in person."

"I'm not going anywhere until I've had my coffee. Is the pot fresh?"

"Ah, well, no, Sheriff. I was just about to make a pot."

"Frank, do you know where the job service office is here in town?"

"I'll have it made in a jiffy, Sheriff, before you know it."

Mo did some paperwork until the coffee was ready. Frank brought him a cup as soon as he finished it. Mo sipped it slowly, delaying his trip to the DA's office as long as possible. He knew what the meeting was about, and he knew he didn't have many options. When his cup was empty, he grabbed his jacket and walked to the door. He turned and, in a raised voice, said, "I'll be in Bob Dooley's office for a while."

He didn't take the cruiser. Dooley's office was just down the street in the courthouse, and he figured the fresh air might let him think more clearly. When he got to the DA's office, he still hadn't thought of any options. He walked in the office and announced to the administrative assistant whose name he couldn't remember, "I'm Sheriff Broussard here to see District Attorney Dooley."

She picked up the phone and told the DA he had arrived. "Go on in," she said, hanging up the phone.

He went in and found Dooley standing behind his desk. Dooley extended his hand and shook Mo's. "Thanks for taking time to come over, Sheriff. I want to talk with you about this missing person case. Have a seat."

Sheriff Mo did as instructed, then said, "What would you like to know, Bob?"

"For starters, tell me about the search of Williams's house. How did that go?"

"There's not much to tell. Special Agent Bevee got a search warrant he asked me to serve to Crease Williams. Bevee and a couple of fellow agents accompanied my deputies and me to the house. Once there, I served the warrant and the agents searched."

"Did you or your deputies impede the search in any way?"

"No, we didn't. What's going on, Bob? You're asking me questions you already have the answers to. It was all in my report."

"I'm getting pressure from a federal level. They want to know why there wasn't an arrest. Frankly, Sheriff, I don't know what to tell them. The search turned up items from the cabin. Why didn't you arrest him?"

"May we talk off the record for a minute?"

"Yes, if it will help sort this out, sure."

"Special Agent Bevee is a smarmy weasel. He's got a personal score to settle with Crease Williams, and he's using this investigation to settle it. I think the search was bogus. I don't think Crease took anything."

"Even if you are right, there's no way to prove that. We have to go on the facts as they appear. Officially, a search turned up stolen items at his residence that belonged to the missing campers. We need to act on that."

"Hell, Bob, we don't even know if a crime has been committed. Those missing guys could show up someplace tomorrow."

"You know how unlikely that is, and besides, theft is a crime. Arrest him for that and suspicion of kidnapping and murder."

"What is that going to solve? I've already instructed him not to leave town or fly. If I arrest him and he posts bail, we'll be right back where we are now."

"That's not entirely true. It'll get the feds off my ass. Plus, I think pressure is being applied in places other than this office. I'm not sure they are going to let him have a reasonable bond. They want him behind bars."

"What's going on here, Bob? I don't get why the feds would be so interested in this case. Bevee can't have that much influence, can he?"

"I don't think so. I believe what you say about Bevee, but the pressure I'm getting is above his pay grade. Mine too. Just get it done."

"I want it understood that I'm doing this under protest."

"Understood."

Chapter 12

The DA hadn't set a deadline for Crease Williams's arrest. Mo knew it would have to be soon. He wanted to make it as pain-free as possible. He would give Beck a call and give her a chance to talk Crease into coming in on his own. The thought of putting him in handcuffs over a bogus search disgusted him.

Beck wasn't happy to hear about the recent development, but it wasn't unexpected. "Did the DA say where the pressure was coming from?"

"Not specifically. He said it was federal pressure."

"I'll talk to Crease. I think I can make him see reason."

"I hoped you would. Don't wait too long."

Beck hung up the phone and tried to come up with the best way to present it to Crease. She knew this was coming, and she knew Crease was aware it was coming. Human nature prevents most people from accepting the inevitable, despite the prior warning, and she was pretty sure Crease was one of those.

She thought she could make his incarceration brief. She knew the court clerk. He was what you might call a nerdy guy. The guy who spent Friday nights playing video games instead of going out on a date in high school. He had always shown obvious, albeit awkward, interest in her. It might cost her one uncomfortable evening, but she figured she could persuade him to juggle the schedule and get Crease's arraignment on the docket quickly.

She didn't waste time. She went to the courthouse immediately, even though the arrest hadn't officially been made. It would be easier to convince Crease to come in on his own if she could give him real expectations. She could have called, but she figured she could be more persuasive in person.

She was right. She got to the courthouse and found the clerk on a break. After ten minutes of explaining the situation, batting her eyes, and showing interest in the little Star Wars figures he had on his desk, the arraignment was on the docket. The spot was as good as she could have hoped for. If she got Crease to come in tomorrow, he would only spend one night in jail.

Cajoling the clerk for a quick court date was the easy part. Convincing Crease was next, and he didn't have any Star Wars figures.

She knocked on his door and pasted on her most alluring smile. When he opened the door, she could see the apprehension on his face. "Hey, Beck, this is a surprise."

"A pleasant one, I hope."

"So do I, but you tell me."

"May I come in?"

"I'm sorry, of course." He opened the door more widely

to allow her to pass. As she did she leaned up and gave him a kiss on the cheek. They both sat down on the sofa. Beck took in a deep breath before she began.

"I have some bad news, but it's just a temporary thing. Sheriff Mo called me today. He said the DA has been getting pressure to have you arrested."

"From Bevee?"

"No, not Bevee. Not directly anyway. He didn't mention any names to me, I don't think he knows himself. The DA just said it was federal pressure."

"And Mo's gonna cave in to that?"

"He doesn't have any choice anymore. You know as well as I do he could have arrested you the day they searched your house. Mo doesn't believe you did anything illegal, but he's backed into a corner. Surely you can see that, right?"

"This is bullshit, Beck. This whole thing is because I was a better football player than Bevee back in college."

"I don't doubt Bevee has an ax to grind, but there's more to it than that. I don't know what's going on exactly, but it's bigger than Bevee and his grudge."

"Even if you're right, I did nothing!"

"I don't doubt that one bit, but I'm not even sure that's the issue. I'm wondering if someone wants you out of the way."

"Out of the way of what?"

"I don't know, Crease, but we're going to find out. For now, though, we need to help Mo out. He's got to arrest you. He has no choice. He could have done it the regular way by coming by without notice and putting you in handcuffs, but he's trying not to do that."

Crease didn't offer any response. She was getting through to him. Time to lay out the plan. "The sheriff is allowing you to come in on your own, no handcuffs, no drama. I'll go with you as your legal representative and your friend. We can wait until tomorrow. That'll give you plenty of time to make whatever preparations you need."

"So how long will I be rotting in jail?"

"That's the best part. I've already contacted the court clerk. He's got the arraignment scheduled the day after tomorrow."

"How is that possible? Aren't courts backed up these days?"

"Yes, but he moved some things around and made it work."

"I'm not even going to ask how you got him to do that."

"I did nothing I'm ashamed of. Green eyes and a little false admiration go a long way with some people." With that, she smiled, and he even smiled back.

"I appreciate you doing that for me."

"I know that. At the arraignment, I'll ask for you to be released on your own recognizance. You have no prior record, and all they have evidence of is theft. It shouldn't be a problem."

"I can't believe this is happening to me."

"I understand, but it's just a small hill we have to climb. One night in jail, and you're out. Then maybe we can figure out what's at the bottom of this."

"You make it sound so simple."

"It will be. Trust me, okay?"

"Sounds like I have little choice in the matter."

"No, not really. How about I take you out for a burger and we'll make a plan. Deal?"

"Deal."

* * *

The next day, as they agreed, Beck picked Crease up at his house an hour before the end of the courthouse business day. This gave the sheriff time to get the arrest on record and would limit Crease's time in jail as much as possible. Beck told the sheriff when to expect them.

They walked across the street together, hand in hand, until they reached the sheriff's office door. After one last gentle squeeze, they released their hands. Beck felt that was the thing to do, given her official capacity.

Sheriff Mo saw them as they walked in the door, and he came around his desk to meet them. Crease, trying to find humor in an uncomfortable situation, said, "I believe you have a reservation for Williams, party of one."

Mo said, "I sure am sorry about this, Crease."

"I know. I don't blame you. Let's just get it over with."

Pointing toward Deputy Joe, Mo said, "If you'll follow Joe into the booking room, he'll get you fingerprinted. While you do that, Beck and I will do the paperwork."

Crease did as instructed, and Beck followed the sheriff into his inner office. Beck sat down across from Sheriff Mo while she watched Crease and the deputy leave the room.

Mo asked her, "How is he taking it?"

"He's doing okay. He understands it's an unpleasant process he must get through."

"We're going to make it as easy on him as we can. They might tell me I have to arrest him, but they didn't tell me how to deal with him. I don't think he's a criminal, so I won't treat him like one."

In the booking room, Joe had just finished the booking pictures. As he and Crease moved to the fingerprint station, Joe asked, "What the hell did you do to this Bevee guy in college?"

"I did nothing to him except make him look bad by comparison."

"Well, he hasn't impressed me much as a federal agent, either, but the man knows how to hold a grudge."

"You know, after he graduated, I never thought I'd see him again, and that would have suited me just fine. Now he's not only back, but he's also trying to destroy my life."

"I know it's a shitty deal right now, but I'll tell ya, Sheriff Mo is not happy one bit. You can bet he will not let this go. He's going to get to the bottom of it."

Beck and the sheriff finished the booking paperwork and Beck asked, "Is there anything else you need from me?"

"No, that's got it. They should be back any minute now if you'd like to wait."

"I don't think so. It might be better if I leave now."

"That's up to you. Don't worry, we'll take good care of him."

"It's nice to know he'll be among friends. I think that makes it bearable for him."

Beck got up to leave and the sheriff rose to shake her hand as she left. A moment later, Joe came back into the room with Crease in tow.

Crease asked, "Is she already gone?"

"She left just a moment ago."

"That's just as well."

Mo turned to Deputy Joe and said, "Go make sure the cell is ready."

"Yes sir, Sheriff."

Mo looked at Crease and said, "I can't believe she got your arraignment scheduled for tomorrow. That little lady is a keeper."

"Yes, she is. She's going to make someone a hell of a wife someday."

"From what I've seen, son, it looks like you've got the market cornered on that front."

"No, not me. Somebody, but not me."

"Why not you?"

"I can't give her the life she deserves."

"What are you talking about? This thing's going to blow over."

"It's not that. Let's not talk about it, okay?"

"Whatever you say, son. Follow me and I'll show you to your accommodations for the evening."

Crease followed Mo down a hallway at the back of the office to a steel door with a sign that read Cells. The sheriff opened the door and held it for Crease. The large room was divided into four identical cells with concrete block walls dividing the two cells on each side. Black iron bars enclosed the front of each one. Every cell had two bunk beds hanging from the walls. Calling them beds was being generous. They were more like steel platforms with an inch or two of vinyl-covered padding on top. Each cell also had a stainless-steel toilet with no seat and a steel lavatory. None of the cells were currently occupied.

"Which one is the presidential suite?" Crease asked.

"We cleaned the first one on the left just for you. If I have your word you won't leave the office, we'll leave the cell door open."

"You have it, and thank you."

"Deputy Jensen will be here in a little while. He'll be manning the office tonight. You may use the restroom at the end of the hall, and there's coffee in the outer office. Help yourself if you want to. Later this evening, Frank will order some dinner from the diner down the street. He's got a menu. When you get sleepy Frank can get you a pillow and blanket if you need it."

"Damn, Sheriff, all the comforts of home."

"We aim to please. Be sure to give us a five-star rating on the travel sites. There's no reason you need to sit back here by yourself. Come on back into the office with me and you can tell me about your little plane ride with Rose."

Crease was more than a little surprised to hear him say that. "So you know about that?"

"There's not much that goes on around town I don't hear about. It's okay, I'm as anxious as you to figure out what's going on here."

The next morning the sheriff had breakfast brought in for Crease. It hadn't been a bad night, all things considered. He didn't think he slept any worse here than he had been at home lately. Beck arrived with the suit she told him to wear at the arraignment. When he was ready, the sheriff led him and Beck to his cruiser and took them to the courthouse.

Once they arrived, Mo took them to a waiting room just off the main courtroom. A person Crease didn't know came in and spoke to Beck quietly for a moment. When she came back to him, she said, "The clerk says they are running ahead of schedule today, so it won't be long."

"That's good. The sooner this is over, the better."

"This should be a quick hearing. It's just a formality for the prosecutor to get the charges on the record. Then I will enter your plea. After that, I'll request you be released until trial, and then we go home."

Crease took a deep breath and let it out slowly. He realized he was wringing his hands and stopped. Beck saw him and said, "Try not to worry. I've done this dozens of times. You won't even have to say anything. Just stand when I do and I'll take care of the rest."

The longer he sat and waited, the harder his heart beat. He had never been in a courtroom before for any reason, let alone charged with a crime.

He waited, but it wasn't long. The clerk came back into the room and looked at Beck. She got up, so he did as well. She smiled at him and walked toward the door. He followed her, making sure not to fall too far behind as if he might get lost between the waiting area and the courtroom.

They walked through the side door of the courtroom, and he could see the courtroom was just what he expected after seeing dozens of courtroom dramas on TV over the years. There was a raised judge's desk with a large office chair. A space of floor in front of that was interrupted by two long wooden desks that faced the judge's desk. Behind those was a short wooden rail with a swinging gate in the middle, between the two lawyers' tables. There were seats, more like church pews really, about ten rows deep and only sparsely populated today.

Beck walked to the closer of the two lawyer's tables, on the left facing the judge. She opened her briefcase and removed some papers and a folder. Then sat down. He sat quietly in the chair next to her.

In a few moments, the back door of the courtroom opened and the District Attorney Robert Dooley came walking down the aisle. He came through the gate and set his briefcase on the table opposite Crease and Beck. Crease didn't know the man, other than by reputation. He'd seen him around town a few times, but Crease was pretty sure they didn't socialize in the same circles.

Once the DA got his papers organized the way he wanted them, he picked up one set of papers and came walking over toward Beck. He leaned over to speak to Beck in a low voice. In spite of that Crease was just able to make out his words as he said, "Ms. Larmar, I'm sorry to tell you this, but I'll be adding a charge today, suspicion of murder."

This appalled Beck obviously, and she protested, "You don't have any evidence to support that."

"Maybe not enough to convict, but enough to bring the charge. I'll also be requesting remand until trial." He handed Beck the papers he was holding, walked back to his table and sat down.

Beck began reading the papers the DA had handed her. Crease leaned in and whispered, "I heard what he said, but what does remand mean?"

Beck stopped reading and looked at him. "That means he will oppose you being released until the trial. That would have been ridiculous when the charge was only theft, but with this new suspicion of murder charge, he could get it. Our plan hasn't changed. You just stand when I do, and otherwise, let me handle it."

Crease's head was spinning when the judge came through the back door. The bailiff said, "All rise." Crease did but on rubber legs. When the bailiff said who was presiding, it didn't even register with Crease. He couldn't have repeated the judge's name if his life depended on it.

The next few minutes passed with Crease in a fog. He heard the DA say something about waving the reading, and then the judge said, "How do you plead?" Beck stood up and said, "The defendant pleads not guilty to all charges." That statement jarred him back to reality.

The judge said, "Well, it sounds like we will have

ourselves a trial. The clerk will look at the schedule and find an opening. Knowing how backed up my schedule is, I'm sure it will be several weeks in the future at least. What shall we do with Mr. Williams in the meantime?"

The DA immediately stood up and said, "Your Honor, given the seriousness of the charges, the people request the defendant be remanded until trial."

Beck stood up when she replied and said, "Your Honor, I've seen the evidence. There's not enough to support the charge of murder. Mr. Williams is an upstanding member of the community with steady employment. He has no prior record at all. We request he be released on his own recognizance."

The judge seemed to ponder both declarations and said, "I think given the charges, recognizance isn't indicated. However, I don't like to hold defendants for lengthy periods before trial without overwhelming evidence, which I don't see here. I will release the defendant with bail in the amount of two hundred and fifty thousand dollars. Next case."

Beck slumped into her chair and hung her head. Crease was confused. He asked her, "What's wrong? I got released, didn't I?"

"Only if you have twenty-five thousand dollars to pay a bondsman."

"I don't. I mean, I'm not doing that. I'll put the bail up myself."

"You're going to post your own bond of two hundred fifty thousand dollars?"

"I get it back, right? As long as I show up?"

"Yes."

"Okay then. I know I'm collecting problems like it's a new hobby, but money isn't one of them. Just call the accounting firm of Bates and Beasley. I told them you were my attorney and I might need money transferred today. They'll be ready."

Beck didn't know what to say. She was happy but dumbfounded at the same time. She took the piece of paper Crease handed her with the accountant's number on it and headed for the clerk's office.

Sheriff Mo waited until they had completed the money transfer so he could take Beck and Crease back to his office, where Beck's car was parked. Beck's initial happiness after discovering Crease could post his own bail was replaced with anger and frustration.

As they climbed into the sheriff's cruiser, Beck said, "I'm sorry, Crease, I didn't see that coming. They caught me completely flat-footed with the suspicion of murder charge."

Crease, trying to quell her frustration, said, "It's okay, Beck. I'm out. Everything worked out fine, just like you said it would."

"No, it's nothing like I said it would be. You're facing a murder charge, four of them, actually, and you had to pony up two hundred fifty thousand dollars, just to stay out of jail. What if you couldn't have done that? What then? You'd have been in jail for months, and I wasn't prepared for it."

Sheriff Mo tried to reassure her. "You couldn't have seen it coming. It makes little sense. They have nothing to support murder charges. Hell, we still don't know what happened to those guys. They could be camping out in a cave somewhere for all we know."

Beck responded, "You know the DA as well as I do. I have my differences with him, but he strikes me as a talented attorney. He's never thrown charges at a defendant unsupported by the evidence before. Not that I've seen."

Sheriff Mo responded, "You are right. I've never seen him do that before, either. That's why you need to stop beating yourself up about it. You couldn't have seen it coming, because they don't have a case to support it."

"Okay, fine. So I couldn't have seen it coming. We both agree the DA doesn't bring frivolous charges, so what's going on?"

"We know the DA was getting pressure from someone. I don't know who exactly, but it was federal. That's got to be why he added the suspicion of murder charge. So what is the feds' interest in this? Bevee is a fed, and we know he has a grudge to pursue with Crease. Is that all it's about? A pissed-off FBI guy trying to even a score?"

"It can't be that simple. He would need support from above. He couldn't orchestrate this by himself."

After listening to Beck and Mo going back and forth, Crease finally said, "What about the structure Rose and I found? Whatever it is was probably the thing that camper wrote about in his journal. Don't you think there's a connection between that and Bevee, and maybe all the federal pressure? Maybe they are trying to hide something, or keep it hidden."

Beck said, "That fits. They want to keep something hidden and so they wanted you tucked away in jail. That would explain why they brought felony charges. They didn't think you'd post bond. They would lock you up and stop you from snooping around."

Mo thought about what she said for a moment, then said, "Yeah, but it would only be temporary. They couldn't make the murder charges stick, not with what they have for evidence."

"You are right, but think about it. What happens to an investigation once someone is charged and brought to trial?"

Mo thought a moment and said, "Nothing."

"Exactly. Nothing happens. The investigation comes to a stop. The prosecutor claims the defendant beat the charges. They never admit they might have made a mistake and charged the wrong person. So there's no reason to further the investigation. It just stops. That's what they want. They don't care if Crease is found innocent or guilty as long as the investigation stops."

"If that is true, we need to know a lot more about what's out there in the forest. Whatever is there must be the reason for this whole thing. The charges against Crease, the reappearing journal, the disappearance, all of it."

Crease said, "We flew over the place twice. We couldn't see much. Short of hiking up there, how are we going to see more?"

After a moment of silence, Mo said, "I've got a thirteen-year-old nephew who might be of some help."

Chapter 13

When Crease first moved to town, he went into Owens Family Food Market because it was close to his house. The first time he shopped there, he discovered they carried a brand of tamales he had only seen in Fort Worth. They were a staple item when he was growing up and finding them here made him a regular customer.

It was a smallish mom-and-pop establishment that had been in business for years, long before Crease came to town. The store didn't offer a large variety of brands like the major national chain markets, but they stocked everything he was looking for. There were only a handful of employees in the store, and the owner, Gina Owens, could be found running a register most days.

At Gina's side, or at least in the general vicinity, would be her little daughter, Christina, a bright and well-mannered six-year-old who had a rare genetic malady that had gradually taken the use of her legs in the time Crease had known her. It had gotten so serious she could no longer walk on her own. For a while, Gina would give her a stool to sit on where she would have to stay while her mom was busy working.

A couple of weeks ago, however, Christina started using an electric wheelchair, one specially made for a child of her size. It was an item Gina couldn't afford, but it had been ordered by a local medical supply company. The company wouldn't say who had paid for the specialized chair, and Crease liked it that way.

Today was the first time he had been in the store since the wheelchair had appeared. As he was checking out, Christina, who was beaming with a smile from ear to ear, waved vigorously.

"Hi, Mr. Crease, did you see my new chair? I'll race you to the door!"

"That's a pretty nice chair. I think you'd beat me, sweetie."

"Yeah, I probably would. I love my chair. I can go anywhere I want to now. Mom said an angel brought it, but it was really the UPS man. I saw him."

Crease knelt down to her level and said, "That's just about the best chair I've ever seen." Christina gave him a guided tour of how her chair worked, including a demonstration of her going to the door and back.

Gina scanned the last of his purchases and said, "There's not much on your grocery list today, Crease."

"No, I've got a lot going on. I don't know how much time I'll have to cook at home."

"I understand. It's a small town. I've heard rumors about your situation."

"I'll bet I'm the talk of the town these days." Nodding

toward Christina, Crease added, "How's she doing? Have you found out anything new?"

Gina knitted her fingers together and placed her hands over her chest. "There is a new treatment that is very promising. She is an excellent candidate for the treatment."

"That's wonderful! How long will it take?"

"It's not that simple. It's an experimental treatment only available at Wexner Medical Center in Columbus, Ohio. We can't afford to travel there or the cost of treatment, even if we did. The insurance won't cover the cost of treatment because it's experimental."

"If I remember correctly, I graduated with a young lady who is now on the medical staff in that center. I'd be happy to call her and just see if there are any options for getting Christina in for treatment. No promises, but it might be worth a call."

"Oh, Crease, if you don't mind doing that, it would be great. I understand it probably won't come to anything, but just to have hope would be great for a while."

"I'm happy to do it. I'll be back in here sometime later this week. I'll try to have something to tell you by then."

"Thank you so much, Crease. I'll try not to get my hopes up too high."

Crease paid for his groceries, waved goodbye to Christina, and walked out of the store. As he was walking to his car, he was telling himself he hadn't actually lied to her. He was sure he graduated with some young ladies who were premed, and maybe one of them ended up at Wexner. It was possible. It was only a little white lie. There would, of course, have to be another little white lie when he talked with her again, but he could live with that. He'd call that medical center in the morning and get things rolling for Christina.

***

Three o'clock in the morning was a time of fervent activity around the landing field by Half Moon Outfitters. The wee hours of the morning, when a dark night was at its darkest, were when the nocturnal creatures of the forest vie for attention, each one sounding off in the manner given it. Chirping, singing, croaking, groaning, and growling made the forest alive with sound.

Three o'clock was when Crease told Gina to arrive at the field. Taking off then would give them plenty of time to land in Columbus and take a taxi to the medical center. The doctors would complete the treatment in one day, and they would keep Christina another day for observation. If there were no problems, he would fly back, pick up Christina and her mom, and bring them home.

When he spoke to Gina after his call to the medical center, he tried to keep the lies to a minimum. While it was true the lying was with the best of intentions, his mom brought him up to be honest always, and so it rubbed against his grain. He had told Gina, with the help of a contact at Wexner, that they accepted Christina into the experimental treatment program. That was kind of true, true enough for his purposes anyway. He told her she shouldn't talk about it with anyone at the medical center because someone might get in trouble.

His last lie was the big one. He told her there would be no charge for the treatment or hospital stay because Christina fit a profile they needed to complete the trial. Actually, he had spoken to the center's billing department and connected them with the firm of Bates and Beasley, the accountants who managed the money his parents left him. All bills were to be sent directly to them. If things went as planned, and with a little luck, Gina would never know who had really paid for the treatment.

Gina arrived on time with a very excited Christina in tow. When he had told them the plan to get to the medical center, Christina exclaimed, "We're going to fly in a plane! Are you going to fly it yourself, Mr. Crease?" He had told her he would, which made him a superhero in her eyes.

He got their luggage all packed away before helping them into the Cessna. He got Christina belted into a back seat before helping Gina into the copilot chair. As he reached out his hand for her, she instead hugged him and with tears running down her cheeks, whispered, "Thank you so much."

He smiled and returned the hug. "Hey, I never miss a chance to land at a new airport."

She laughed and said, "How can I ever repay you for this?"

"Heck, it's just a plane ride. Make me a deal on those tamales I like."

"You've got it. Tamales on the house from now on."

"That's a deal!"

He helped her into the plane and went around and got in himself. The flight was uneventful. Despite the smooth ride, Christina didn't sleep a wink. She had her nose pressed against the window any time they passed over a small town with streetlights.

They landed at a small airport in Columbus just as the sun was coming up. They took a cab to Wexner Medical Center, where Crease helped them find the building where they checked in. As he watched Christina being placed into a wheelchair, he said a silent prayer to himself. Just before they disappeared into an elevator, Christina waved vigorously, and Gina looked at him and clutched both hands to her heart.

Chapter 14

Mo called Crease and Rose and asked them to be in his office at one o'clock. Beck was with Crease when he took the call, so she came along for good measure. Rose was already there when Crease arrived with Beck in tow. Crease wasn't sure Beck had ever met Rose, so he introduced them.

After the introductions, Rose said, "So you are the young thing trying to steal the heart of my man." She said it with a wink and a smile.

"I'll admit I've been trying, but I'm not sure how successful I've been."

"You hang in there. He's a tough fish to land. I've been trying for years."

Crease, a little embarrassed, said, "Can you two stop talking about me like I'm not in the room?"

Under her breath, Rose said, "I'll take you to lunch sometime, girl, and I'll give you some pointers. I've landed more than a few men in my time. I married two of them, but they weren't in it for the long haul. Their alimony checks still clear, though."

"That sounds like an interesting lunch date. Let's do it."

Just then, Sheriff Mo came in from the booking room and motioned for them all to follow him back there. Crease noticed they had rearranged things right away since they booked him a few days ago. A desk in the corner displayed a laptop computer and a color laser printer. A boy who looked like he was just entering puberty sat in an office chair in front of the desk.

Mo was standing between the boy and the group. "Crease, Beck, Rose, I'd like you to meet Jeffery. He is my nephew on my wife's side. Jeffery's hobby is searching satellite images online for unusual things. He's found some stuff in the last couple of years that I couldn't explain. I'm hoping he might help us identify what Rose saw from the air the other day."

Crease said, "If we couldn't see much of it flying close to the ground, why do you think a satellite image would be better?"

"It might not be any better, but Jeffery tells me satellite images these days are very detailed. Plus, they take pictures with the satellite directly over the site. That might be better than you looking out the plane window from an angle where you have to look through the surrounding trees. I figured it was worth a try. Did you bring the GPS coordinates you wrote?"

Crease reached into his pocket and brought out a piece of paper. "Yes, I've got them. If he can find anything on a satellite image, it has to be more than we saw, I suppose. Rose couldn't even glimpse it long enough to take a picture.

All we know is something is there."

Mo handed the paper to Jeffery, who read it and started typing on the laptop keyboard. A couple of minutes later Jeffery said, "Uncle Mo, this is the area that came up with your coordinates."

Crease and Rose gathered around the desk with Mo to look at the image on the laptop.

"I see nothing but trees," Crease said as he looked.

Jeffery said, "We'll have to scroll around some. The coordinates get you close, but it's just an area."

Jeffery scrolled the screen a little at a time, giving Rose a chance to look at the screen. Every image looked the same. There wasn't anything in the area but trees, and they all looked alike.

After a few more scrolls, Rose's eyes lit up. "There! Do you see it?" Crease and Mo looked hard, but only saw trees. "Right there, between those trees. Something is there."

Still failing to see anything, Mo asked Jeffery, "Can you zoom in on that area she's pointing to?"

Jeffery clicked the mouse a few times, and the image of the trees got closer. Crease and Mo leaned in close. Finally, Crease said, "Yes, I see something. I can't tell what it is, but it's underneath the trees."

Beck asked Jeffery, "Do you know what time of year this image was taken?"

Before Jeffery could answer, Mo said, "What difference does that make? Pine trees are green year-round. They don't drop all their needles in winter."

"No, pine trees don't, but deciduous conifers do."

"Digi-what? What are you talking about, Beck?"

"Deciduous conifers are a species of tree that isn't evergreen. They drop all their needles in winter. We have them in the forest around here. If Jeffery can find an image taken in winter, it might make things easier to see."

Jeffery said, "They took this image in June. I'll see if I can find a different one."

While Jeffery was looking, Mo said, "Where did you learn so much about trees?"

Beck said, "I don't know. You pick things up as you go along."

Jeffery looked through image after image and eventually came upon one he thought might be better. "Here's one that was taken the year before, in February. I'll scroll and try to find the same place."

Jeffery scrolled, and Rose looked on intently. He stopped at the location he thought had shown something before. Trees and brush were all Rose could see. Jeffery backed the image off. It made everything smaller, but it increased the size of the area in all directions.

Rose looked hard, taking in the whole screen. Then she leaned forward, and pointing to the upper-right corner of the screen, said, "There. Can you zoom in right there?" Jeffery scrolled so the place Rose was pointing to was at the center of the screen. Then he zoomed into it as much as he could without distorting the image.

"That's it," Rose said. "It's still covered with trees, but you can see more of it now."

Crease moved closer to the desk to see for himself. Pine trees still covered much of it, but there was enough visible to see that it wasn't just a structure, but a solid building. It was still difficult to judge the size, and Crease wondered if part of it might be underground.

Mo was looking at the screen as well. "Look at that area just to the left of the building."

Crease asked, "What about it? It just looks like more trees."

"Yes, but look all around the image. Everywhere else there are some trees, the ones Beck told us about, that are bare. There are some of them everywhere except that area to the left of the building."

"Yes, I see it now. That area looks different from everywhere else. What are you thinking, Mo?"

"No roads lead up there and it isn't close to the lake. There would have been a lot of stuff brought in to build that place. It must have come in by air. I think that area beside the building isn't trees at all. I think it's a helicopter landing area that someone camouflaged to look like trees from the air."

"Now that you say that, I see what you mean. It's too uniform compared to everywhere else. How does that help us?"

"I'm not sure it does. It is an interesting bit of knowledge to tuck away, though."

"This has got to be what interested the campers. Is there any way to learn what that building is being used for?"

Mo replied sarcastically, "We could just ask your friend Bevee to give us a tour of the place."

"Are you convinced Bevee and this place are connected?"

"That makes the most sense to me."

"Okay, now we know what the campers were interested in, and we think it involves Bevee. We still don't know what it is. What is our plan?"

Mo answered, "I don't have one. Beck, do you have any ideas?"

She replied, "No, not at the moment, but this is good. We've made progress. I think we should take some time to mull it over and meet again later."

Everyone nodded in agreement.

The night was more restful than Crease had experienced in a while. Maybe finding an image of something in the woods had eased his mind. Whatever the reason, it felt good to have a restful night again. He lay in the morning's peacefulness, the sun just lifting the darkness from around him. He listened to the chirping of the early birds at the first glimpse of morning light.

Then there was a noise. Not a loud noise. In fact, a quiet one, but human. When that fact registered in his brain, he bolted up to a sitting position.

"Easy there, cowboy. If we wanted to hurt you, it would have already happened."

Crease's eyes struggled to focus on the source of the voice. They found a shadowy figure sitting at the foot of his bed. Another figure stood behind the first. As his eyes adjusted, he could make out a few details. Both men wore typical business attire, including suit coats and ties.

"How the hell did you get in here? Who do you work for?"

"Questions. Everyone in your position always asks the same questions. The answers don't matter. What does matter is that we're here, and we've been watching you sleep for twenty minutes. We left you undisturbed, dreaming whatever people like you dream about. It could have gone differently, that's what matters."

"What do you want?"

"There you go again with the useless questions. I want a fifty-foot yacht and season tickets to the Vikings games, but that doesn't matter. What matters is what my employers want, or more precisely, what they don't want. They don't want you. They don't want you meddling into things that are none of your concern."

"They made it my concern when they planted evidence to get me arrested."

"You'll beat those charges. I know about that sweet little attorney of yours. She's the total package. Good looks and smart too. She'll get you out of it."

"Consider the arrest as a warning buoy, using naval vernacular. A warning that you are sailing into dangerous waters and should adjust your heading. Jones and me, sitting here in the wee hours of the morning, having this pleasant conversation with you, let's call this a shot across the bow. You only get one of those.

"What happens now is up to you. Stop searching, questioning, and talking about things that aren't your business. If you do that, you'll never see me again. If you don't, then what happens next is up to me. We might come back and visit you again. Are you thinking about keeping a gun or knife under your pillow? Go ahead. We'll kill you with it. That'll give your friend the sheriff an interesting murder case to solve. That's not the only option. Maybe you will disappear just like those campers, and no one ever sees you again. The same thing could happen to that sweet little attorney. Have I answered your questions now?"

Crease, angry, said, "How about you get the hell out of my house!"

"He's talking tough. I like it when they talk tough, don't you, Jones?" His companion offered no response. "Jones doesn't talk much. We'll leave quietly, the same way we came in. Don't make us come back."

The figure sitting at the foot of his bed got up, and both

men left the room. He heard the back door close. Crease watched out the window but never saw them get into a vehicle.

After Crease got his wits back, he walked through the house to convince himself they were no longer there. They were gone. There was no reason for them to hang around. They did what they came to do. They scared him. When he thought about it, he was more angry than scared. They hadn't only threatened him. They threatened Beck too.

He wasn't sure how to proceed. After losing his family and his future, he had begun a new life. He never allowed people to become too close. He didn't want to mourn for anyone again. He had made a good life for himself until now. He was pretty sure that was over. He didn't know what to do next, but he thought back to a football game his dad took him to, years ago.

For as long as he could remember, his dad took him to see the Cowboys play. They didn't go to all the home games, but they saw four or five every year. If you lived in the Dallas area, it was hard not to be a Dallas Cowboys fan. If you grew up watching them play, there was almost no way to be a fan of any other team.

When Crease was very young, he didn't really understand there were teams to cheer for other than the Cowboys. In his young outlook on the world, there were the Cowboys and a group of random teams that came to town to play against them. The names of these teams didn't matter. They only existed to play the Cowboys.

As he got older, his father explained who these teams were. He explained the whole regular season and playoff process. By October 5th, 2003, he understood everything concerning NFL conferences, who the Cowboy's biggest rivals were, and common football rules. He probably knew as much as any avid fan by that date. Why his father chose that date, and that game, to teach him some life lessons, he would never know.

Jacob began where he had left off, "After a string of losing seasons the owners of the Cowboys franchise decided to sell the team. They considered several offers and settled on the one from Jerry Jones, an Arkansas businessman with some college football experience. He had big plans for the team and started making changing things right away. One of the first things he did was fire the legendary coach Tom Landry. He could see Landry wasn't keeping up with the rest of the league. It wasn't a popular decision with the fans but he was right to do it. He brought in a college coach he had known for many years, Jimmy Johnson. Johnson was just what the team needed: a tough coach with new ideas. Johnson made big changes, and in just a couple of years he molded the team into a Super Bowl contender."

Crease hated to interrupt the monologue, but in an effort to show he was paying attention, he said, "Yes, I remember you telling me how great the team was when I was born. They won two championships in a row, right?"

"That's right, 1992 and '93. Then again in 1995. It was quite an accomplishment. After that, however, things went downhill fast."

"What happened?"

"After the first two Super Bowl victories, everyone heralded Jimmy Johnson as a genius. Taking a team from a one-win season to an NFL champion in such a short time had never been done before. As wonderful as winning the Super Bowl was, the team owner, Jerry Jones, was jealous of Jimmy Johnson's success. There was friction between them and ultimately Johnson quit the team. They won the 1995 Super Bowl after he left, but with the team he had assembled.

"After Jimmy Johnson left, Jerry Jones took over the team-building operations and proclaimed himself to be not only team owner, but the general manager as well. The general manager is the person primarily responsible for assessing player talent, selecting players in the annual college draft, and assembling a winning team."

"I'll be the first to say that Jerry Jones is a terrific businessman. He knows how to make money. He is one of the most successful team owners in NFL history. The value of the franchise has quadrupled since he bought it."

"He is not a good general manager. Since the 1995 season, the Cowboys have only been average. Elite teams begin with a general manager who knows his job. Talented players graduate college every year, and the top prospects are obvious. Anyone can find those players. What makes a great general manager, and in turn, a great team, is finding talented players that aren't on everyone's scouting report. Jerry Jones isn't that guy, and as long as he insists on filling a role he has no talent for, the Cowboys will not return to another Super Bowl.

"That is another lesson to take away from today. Know your limitations. Make the most of the talents you have, but realize you can't do everything yourself. Be humble enough to allow other people to help you. Outstanding success is rarely the result of one individual. It almost always requires a team effort."

It was a lesson Crease took to heart back then. It made sense throughout his high school years and into college. Football was all about team effort. No matter how good a player a person is, it requires all his teammates doing their job for him to be successful.

After the death of his parents, teamwork made little sense anymore. Good teams required closeness, and he wanted no part of that. Being close to people leaves you susceptible to personal pain. It sets you up for heartache. He'd had enough heartache.

Now, however, he had just experienced something he figured very few people ever would. Waking up in the early morning with men sitting, watching you sleep. He knew the reason they threatened him that way was to show just how vulnerable he was. They succeeded. What should he do now?

He could do what they asked and stop questioning or searching for answers. If they did not convict him, that might be the end. Except that would end all investigation. Whatever happened to those campers would likely never come to light. He hated the thought of that. The possibility the government thugs would make good on their threat didn't matter. He didn't believe Beck was in any danger. They would gain nothing from that. It was just another method of intimidation. Would they try to kill him? Maybe, but he had little future either way.

He knew he wouldn't be successful in resolving this situation on his own. He doubted there would be a satisfactory result no matter what he did. His best chance of surviving was to bring everyone together, share information and ideas, and plan a strategy. He had people who cared about him; he knew that. He cared about them, too, despite his efforts not to. It was time to toss the loner mentality, at least to a point.

The logical first step was to go see Mo. To tell him what happened and discuss the possibility of bringing everyone together. All the people who had any connection with this situation. They needed a big brainstorming session.

He thought Mo would be good with that.

Crease was about to do what he didn't do anymore. He would ask for help.

The sheriff's cruiser was parked on the street, so Crease figured Mo would be in his office. He wanted to get things out while they were fresh on his mind. As if waking up to men threatening to kill you would be something a person would forget. He laughed to himself at that thought.

He walked into the sheriff's office and looked around for a second. He could see Sheriff Mo was sitting behind his desk reading something. He didn't wait for an invitation. He walked into the sheriff's inner office and closed the door behind him. Mo looked up from the papers he was holding and said, "Hey, Crease, I was just thinking about you."

"Mo, we need to talk."

"Okay, pull up a chair."

Crease sat in one of the two chairs facing Mo's desk and drew in a long breath. "I had visitors last night. Two men came into my house before sunrise and were at the foot of my bed when I woke up this morning."

"Damn, son, that's a pretty dramatic way to start your day."

"Yes, it is, but I don't recommend it."

"Let me guess. Well-dressed gentlemen, rather large, one of them named Jones?"

"That's right. How did you know?"

"They stopped by for a friendly chat with me earlier today. At least they didn't get me out of bed. They told you to stop asking questions?"

"They strongly suggested it."

"I was told you are the guy and to leave it at that. If I

keep investigating, I'll find myself out of a job and up to my eyeballs in IRS audits."

"Hell, they only threatened me with death."

They both laughed at that comment. After a brief silence, Crease said, "It feels good to laugh. I haven't had a good laugh in a very long time. All kidding aside, the well-dressed gentlemen struck me as being serious about the threats."

"Yes, I think they meant business. Which means the ball is in our court and I don't mind telling you being threatened to keep me from doing my job pisses me off."

"I feel the same way. I'm a Texas boy. We don't respond well to threats."

"Bayou folks don't either. Sounds like we both agree to say to hell with the threats. That said, do we have a plan for moving forward?"

"I don't have any specific plan, but after those two smarmy types left, I thought about something my father taught me. He said outstanding success was rarely the work of an individual. It usually involves a team effort."

"I'll go along with that, so what do you have in mind?"

"I think we should bring everyone who has had a part of this case together. Then lay out the entire story for the group. Rose, Beck, Deputy Pride, and Deputy Jensen have all had their part in this. Let's fill them all in about everything we know. It might generate some ideas we haven't thought about."

"Don't forget Ol' Pete."

"I'm not sure Pete knows what's been going on."

"Don't underestimate Pete. He knows more than you think."

"Okay then, we'll bring Pete into it as well."

Sheriff Mo thought to himself and nodded at the idea. "Whatever we do, it must be quick and decisive. These guys are serious about making you disappear."

"As sheriff, can you bring everyone together quietly?"

"I'm sure I can make that happen."

Chapter 15

Crease left it for Sheriff Mo to determine where and when to hold this hopeful meeting. Crease felt it was time to have a serious conversation with Beck about the limits of the relationship that was obviously developing between them.

He believed the best chance for a positive resolution to the current situation was to reach out to people, Beck included. The personal relationship he and Beck had was different. There was a limit on how far he could allow it to grow. It was time to explain things to her. Things he'd told no one before.

He took her to the only restaurant in the area that had a discreet atmosphere. The Shady Inn had a piano bar, and the clientele was mostly middle-aged couples having a night out. White linen tablecloths and candles adorned each table. The wait staff dressed semiformally in black slacks and white button-down shirts. The dim lighting encouraged quiet conversation.

A gently sloping, curving walkway led from the parking lot to the building. Meandering through shrubs and ornamental trees, ground-level sconces lit the way. As they began the walk to the building, hand in hand, Beck said, "I've never been here before."

"No, neither have I," Crease replied.

"I guess that makes this a special occasion."

They stepped up to the hostess's table and Crease said they had a reservation for two. The hostess picked up two menus and said, "Right this way."

They followed her to a table along the large, wall-sized window facing the garden. She pulled out a chair for Beck and then Crease. She handed them each a menu and told them James would be their server.

They opened their menus briefly before James was there to take their drink orders. When they returned to perusing their menus, Beck said, "Oh my, this is a rather expensive place."

"Order anything you like. I've told you before, money is not one of my problems."

"As displayed by your willingness to put up two hundred fifty thousand dollars for your bail. I have to tell you, I was quite shocked by that."

"Yes, I know, but it isn't like I spent the money. You said I will get it back after I show up for court, right?"

"Yes, that's right. Still, most people don't have that kind of money sitting around somewhere."

"My father was a good planner and a good businessman. I'm the beneficiary of his efficiency."

"Well, here's to your father." She raised her glass and he touched it with his own. They both took a sip just before James came back to the table.

"I can recommend the prime rib for two. It's a house specialty."

Crease looked at Beck and she nodded. Crease said, "That will be fine. We'll have two Cesar salads as well."

"Very good, sir."

James collected the menus and left the table. When he was out of earshot, Crease asked, "Has Sheriff Mo called you yet?"

"Yes, I heard from him today. He said he is bringing everyone who's had anything to do with your case together for a meeting."

"He didn't say why?"

"No, not specifically."

"It was my idea. He and I were both visited by a couple of gentlemen who were very interested in stopping any more investigation of this case."

"What does 'very interested' mean?"

"Without going into all the details, they basically said our lives were at risk. Well, my life, his financial stability. Neither of us wants to cave in to smarmy musclemen making threats. I told him it might be a good idea to bring everyone in to have a kind of brainstorming session."

"Do you think you are in real danger?"

"If we don't handle this right, yeah, I think so."

"Why not stop then? Why take such a chance?"

"For several reasons. I don't like being threatened. I don't like being accused of something I didn't do. I think there may be something going on up by Half Moon Lake that the government and Agent Bevee are trying to hide. Those are the primary reasons, but there are other, more personal ones."

"It all makes me very nervous. I didn't realize the

people we are dealing with would take it to this level."

"Come and meet with Mo and help us deal with this situation. Who knows? We may not have any options, but we want to find something if possible. Now let's change the subject. How about this weather we're having?"

That made Beck laugh, which was the point. With the threats so real and so fresh in their minds, it was difficult to think of anything else, but Beck found a new topic.

"You've told me about your family life when you were young. Why are you an only child?"

The question surprised him. He couldn't remember ever being asked about that before. He thought briefly and said, "I don't know the answer to that question. I'm not sure there is an answer. When I was young, I never thought to ask. That's just the way it was. I was a happy child, and my parents seemed to be happy. I don't know if there was a physical issue or a conscious decision to only have me. Looking back now, I wish I had asked. It would be nice now to have siblings to share life with. I'd like to have some family."

"There are ways to create a family for yourself."

Just then, James arrived with the prime rib for two. Crease was grateful for the interruption. The conversation was heading where he needed it to go, but he was happy to put it off as long as possible. James served both of them and asked if either of them needed another drink or anything else. Crease asked for another beer, hoping that would make the upcoming conversation easier.

The prime rib was excellent, and for a time they focused on only that. It didn't last. Once pleasant frivolous conversation trailed off, he decided it was time. "You mentioned earlier about creating a family for myself. You need to know something about me."

"That sounds ominous."

"Yes, I'm sorry. It's just that I've told no one what I'm about to tell you."

"Okay. I don't know how to respond to that. I'll listen to whatever you have to say, but it won't change the way I feel about you."

"After my parents died in the accident, I lost interest in the life I had been living. They were such a large part of it, I couldn't imagine going on the same way without them. I gave up football and looked for a place to move far away from all the memories in Texas. I found this place. I took flying lessons and got a job flying floatplanes."

Beck broke in and said, "You've told me a lot of this. I know what you did."

"Yes, but there's more."

"Okay."

"When I got here, I didn't want to make close friends, and so I've kept to myself these past years. I've made some acquaintances, but I've not allowed anyone close. I've been a loner. I didn't want to be hurt again."

Beck said, "I can understand that. That's nothing to be ashamed about."

"I'm not ashamed of it. That's just the way it's been. Until those two goons paid me a visit. It made me think back to something my dad had told me years ago. That you can't do everything on your own. Success comes from team efforts. That's when I asked Mo to bring everyone to a meeting."

"So you're coming around to embracing friends. That's good."

"Yes, I think it is. I think I have to if there's any way of getting through this case. That's not the entire story, however." Crease paused long enough to take a drink of his beer, then continued. "Do you know that before you and I started spending time together, I hadn't had a date since I left Texas?"

"No, I did not."

"There is a reason for that, and it goes deeper than choosing to be a loner. Before I continue, however, I think I should ask a question. Is there a 'thing' between us? I mean something beyond a dinner out like this? As I said, I haven't dated in years, so maybe my senses have dulled."

"In the first place, it may surprise you to learn that I date little more than you have."

"Yes, that surprises me."

"I've never been into dating just for fun. So you and I seeing each other as much as we do is my way of letting you know you mean something to me. More than anyone ever has before. Is that what your senses have been telling you?"

"Pretty close."

"My senses tell me you feel the same way. Am I wrong?"

"You aren't wrong. That's what makes the rest of my story so difficult to tell. I was being scouted heavily by the NFL. My dad thought it would be a good idea to have my DNA tested. It was becoming a big thing then. There was even talk about the NFL making it mandatory. Of course, that never happened, but at the time Dad thought we should get ahead of the game."

"I remember that. There was a big public debate about DNA testing and privacy. Privacy prevailed."

"Yes, but that was long after my test. After my parent's funeral, I had to go through everything: the will, insurance policies, and all the other papers a person has to find after the death of their parents."

"You came across your DNA results?"

"I did. I don't know how long my father had the report before he died, but he waited to tell me. Maybe he didn't want to ruin my year with us looking at a bowl game that season. I don't know. So I read it for myself. From a football perspective, the results were normal. The test didn't end there, however. They tested for everything.

"At first I didn't understand what it was telling me. I had to read it again before the reality set in. It said I have a gene that shows I will suffer from the early onset of Alzheimer's disease. I don't have many years before it happens."

Beck was shocked at first, but then her demeanor calmed. "That just means you are more likely than the average person to have it."

"No, you don't understand. Believe me, I've researched this. Alzheimer's has two types of genetic indicators. One is as you say, indicating a person is more likely to have the disease. The second one, the one I have, only appears in a fraction of one percent of people. Having it means you absolutely will develop Alzheimer's, and at an early age, as young as forty. It isn't just a possibility. It is my future."

Beck had no words to convey how she felt hearing him say that. "I don't know what to say. I'm so sorry." That was all she could muster.

"I know. That's one reason I've told no one. Nobody knows what to say and now that you know I'd like for you to keep it to yourself."

"Of course."

"This is the reason I've avoided dating or building a relationship with anyone. I have no future to offer. I haven't tried to develop the relationship we have either. It just happened."

"I understand that. It was the same for me. It came over me without my knowing about it. I think it was meant to be."

"How could that be true? I have very few years of clear thought left to me. I'm going to lose my mind and then die. I can't believe it was meant for you to endure that."

"That isn't for you to decide. We can't live our lives based on what we think might happen. We must take every day as it comes, and deal with it. I'm not willing to give up what we have because of your DNA test. What did you expect me to say?"

"I didn't really think about it. In my mind, it's a showstopper."

"It isn't. At least not for me. I guess you must decide what you want the most. To continue to live with no chance of family bonds, or not. Life is hard enough with family. Why make it harder than it has to be?"

Her reaction confused him. It was true he hadn't thought about what her reaction would be, but he didn't expect her to be so adamant. So willing to ignore what the future would bring for her.

The rest of the evening, they conversed about trivial things. His mind dwelled on comprehending her reaction and how he would respond to it. Could he choose what his heart wanted, or stick to what his brain always told him was the right thing to do?

Chapter 16

Judging by the number of cars parked along the street, Crease thought everyone must already be in the sheriff's office. He walked in and saw everyone there, sitting around the office wherever there was a chair. Sheriff Mo was standing at the front of the room. When Crease appeared Mo said, "All right, we have everyone now. Let's get started."

Crease remained standing off to the side of the room. He wondered to himself if this was a mistake, bringing everyone into the sheriff's office. If word got out, that might be enough to trigger the worst.

Sheriff Mo spoke confidently as he began talking. "Everyone in the room is aware of the criminal charges against Crease, which are related to the disappearance of the four campers from Roudy's Cabin a while back. You have all had at least a small part of this case. Because of that, I have brought you all together to hear all the facts as we know them, so that maybe as a group we can find a solution.

"Crease and I have been threatened and told to drop any investigation into this case, and I don't think they are bluffing. I guess they thought that would send us running for cover, but I don't respond well to threats. I don't like these people, and I will not cave in to what they are trying to do. The evidence they claimed to find in Crease's home comprised items they picked up themselves to frame him. What's worse is that something they said to Crease shows they are the ones responsible for the disappearance.

"Crease and Rose searched the area north of Roudy's Cabin and found a structure that appears to be at the root of this entire case. We believe the campers stumbled onto whatever is out there, which resulted in their disappearance."

Mo stopped briefly and took a sip of coffee before he continued. "Folks, we are all residents of this small town. Most of us have family here. It's my job as sheriff to protect everyone who lives here. I'm trying to do that, but I need your help. I'd like to hear anything you have to offer, and I will answer questions you have."

The room was silent for a moment while everyone took in everything Mo had just told them.

Ol' Pete was the first to break the silence with a question. "So, Sheriff Mo, these fellas who threatened you, were they government types?"

Mo looked at Crease, who nodded in agreement. "Yes. We think Special Agent Bevee sent them, but we can't prove that."

"That would make this structure connected with the government somehow?"

Mo said, "That would make sense."

Ol' Pete sat back in his chair and said, "I may be able

to shed some light on the situation. Back in a previous life, in the late sixties, I was a member of ICORP in 'Nam. I learned a lot about how our intelligence agencies operate. Most of what they do is under the table, and not necessarily legal. This sounds like one of their operations."

Sheriff Mo broke in. "ICORP in Vietnam? That was decades ago. What makes you think that would apply today?"

"The technology changes and the names change, but the sleaziness remains the same. I got out as soon as I realized what kind of organization I was working for. They take an oath to protect and defend the Constitution, but that's not what they do. They protect the government and themselves, and they don't care who gets hurt in the process."

Crease asked, "So what's your take on what's going on here?"

"To begin with, I'll tell you that Bevee is just the type of guy I used to deal with in 'Nam. He's in it for the glory. He's going to do whatever is in his own best interest. He'll do anything to complete any project they give him. He doesn't think rules and laws apply to him or his agency. Crease says he planted the evidence at his house, and I'm sure that's true."

"He made a mistake, though, and planting evidence was his way of trying to fix it. Except it didn't work, not the way he wanted."

Sheriff Mo said, "What mistake did he make?"

Ol' Pete looked at Crease and said, "Why do you think they chose those three items to plant in your house?"

"The wallets would show me to be a thief, but I'm not sure about the journal. Maybe to discredit me because they removed the entry I read?"

"I think you are pretty close," Pete said. "Bevee planted the wallets because it was something he would have taken. That's the kind of guy he is. The journal and what you read in it is more interesting. This is where I think Bevee made a mistake. The missing entry is the key. It said they saw something interesting they wanted to go back and explore. I think they stumbled on to something that wasn't supposed to be found. Something the government is hiding. I think Bevee knew they found it and went to the cabin to remove any evidence of it."

Crease said, "When would he have done that?"

"I don't know exactly, but the journal disappeared after you delivered supplies, so it would have been sometime between that day and the day you took the sheriff back there. I think his mistake was in thinking he took the journal before anyone saw it. When he found out he was wrong, that you had read it, he had to do something about it. So he got a search warrant for your place and planted it with the wallets."

Sheriff Mo said, "Holy crap. That makes sense, but if you're right, what do you think happened to the campers?"

Pete's expression changed to grim as he said, "I don't know, but if they discovered some secret government project, we likely won't be hearing from them again."

Crease, surprised at Pete's answer, said, "Do you really think the government would go that far?"

"I know you are young, son, but you studied history in school, didn't you? Do you remember reading about the sinking of the *Maine*? The Gulf of Tonkin incident? Those are just two examples where the government sacrificed citizens to get what it wanted. When I say government, I'm not talking about the politicians you vote for on election day. There are agencies in our government run by people nobody elected, and who don't answer to anyone."

Pete turned to Crease and asked, "Is that where you were flying when your plane shut down on you the second time?"

"Yes, Rose and I were looking for something out of place when we found that building."

"This is all making sense now. I checked the device I installed in your plane after you brought it back to me. At first, I thought something was wrong. I couldn't understand what the readings meant. I think I do now. There's nothing wrong with your plane. All the instrumentation, propulsion, sensors, everything shut down at the same time. There's nothing on a plane that singly controls everything. That means the problem had to be external. I think they are doing secret weapons testing. I think they are working on a targeted EMP weapon."

Mo spoke up. "An electromagnetic pulse weapon? I've heard of EMP. It's caused by a nuclear explosion."

"Yes, it is, but the holy grail of weapons development is to generate one without the nuclear explosion. A pulse that could be aimed at an enemy. I think they are testing something just like that up there. When they fire off a test, and you are in the wrong area, that's what caused your plane to shut down. They probably figured testing it way up north surrounded by a forest would keep them hidden and the trees would block a pulse from going too far."

Mo said, "You are right, Pete. Everything you said makes sense. That would sure explain everything. So what can we do about it?"

Beck had been listening intently to everything. "We're

pretty sure we can connect Agent Bevee to this facility?"

Mo answered her. "I think so."

Then Beck continued. "If we could also find evidence showing Bevee had access to the stolen, planted items, it might be enough to get a search warrant for that facility."

"We know he must have taken the stuff from Roudy's Cabin after I delivered the supplies, but before I took Sheriff Mo up there," Crease said. "If Pete is correct, he thought he was collecting anything that would show the campers had found the facility. That's why he took the journal."

"All we need is proof that Bevee had access to Roudy's Cabin during that time," Beck said. "One of my old professors in law school is a federal judge now. He hates government overreach and government agencies that ignore the Constitution. I believe I could convince him to issue a search warrant if we can show Bevee had access to those stolen items in the cabin."

Rose had listened to everything and had a suggestion. "What about DNA evidence? It seems like that solves a lot of crimes these days."

"We don't have any DNA evidence in this case," Mo said.

Beck said, "Maybe not, but how about fingerprints?"

"We lifted fingerprints the day Crease flew us to Roudy's Cabin," Mo said. "We didn't get any matches."

Deputy Pride sat up in his chair. "That's right, Sheriff, but you only had me run the prints against the known criminals database."

Mo said, "Are you sure?"

"Yes sir, I'm sure. At the time that seemed the logical thing to do. We didn't have any reason to look for matches in the federal employees system."

Mo looked at Crease. "The day you took us to the cabin, we went in through the back door, didn't we?"

"Yes, only because that's how I went in when I brought the supplies."

Mo looked at Deputy Pride and said, "That means anyone who came in the front door after you delivered supplies would show fingerprints on the knob. That's our best shot. Deputy Pride, get busy matching prints to the federal database."

"Yes sir, Sheriff."

Mo turned back to Beck. "If we find Bevee's prints, will that be enough evidence? There's no reason for Bevee to have visited that cabin unless he had prior knowledge of what was going on and was looking for something."

"When you put it all together—Bevee's tie to the government, the disappearance of the campers that one henchman referred to while threatening Crease, the journal with one entry removed, and proof Bevee was in the cabin before he should have known anything—I think so," Beck said. "If you find Bevee's prints, I can get you a warrant based upon that."

"Good," Mo said. "You get me the warrant, and I'll serve it. I'll even include an arrest of Agent Bevee for obstruction of justice. Everyone, this has been very helpful. Thank you all for your input. We'll take it from here."

Chapter 17

Without a metropolitan area nearby, internet connections were slow. Looking for a fingerprint match was going to take a while. Crease knew that when the meeting broke up last night. Maybe today he'd get a call from Sheriff Mo with the verdict on the fingerprints.

It was around midday when the phone finally rang and he saw the call was from the sheriff's office. Crease anxiously answered the phone.

"Hello?"

The voice on the line was undoubtedly Sheriff Mo. "Crease? We got it. We found two big fat clear prints on the doorknob that belong to our favorite FBI agent. We found some others in a couple of other places in the cabin as well. This proves he was in Roudy's Cabin before he had any reason to be. Unless he was up to no good."

"That's great news, Mo. Have you passed that information along to Beck yet?"

"I thought I'd let you know first. I'll head over to her office as soon as we hang up."

"That's good. Assuming Beck can get a warrant, have you thought about how you're going to serve it?"

"Some, not a lot. Once I have it in hand, I'll figure something out."

"I'm just thinking out loud here, but it seems serving a search warrant to a group of people who think laws of the land don't apply to them might be difficult."

"It won't be easy, I know that. We will have a plan when the time comes. I want to get this over to Beck. We need to make this happen as quickly as possible. If wind of this gets out, we could wake up to a bad dream that's all too real. We have to act first and fast. That's our only chance of getting through this."

"Okay, Mo, keep me informed."

The sheriff disconnected the phone. Crease knew Beck would work as fast as possible to get a search warrant. That would not make the waiting any easier.

Sheriff Mo brought Beck a folder. It contained the fingerprint analysis that proved Agent Bevee had been in Roudy's Cabin long before he had any reason to be there. It was the smoking gun, the last piece of the puzzle pressed into place to complete the picture of the attempt to frame Crease for the disappearance of the campers.

When Beck was in law school, the professor who had the biggest impact on her development as an attorney was Anthony Wright. Now a federal judge, he held a firm belief in the Constitution as the founding fathers intended it.

He believed their intent was for the government to remain as small as possible, providing a specific group of functions and no more. He agreed with Thomas Jefferson, who said, "When governments fear the people, there is liberty. When the people fear the government, there is tyranny."

He abhorred the continuous expansion of government authority and felt it was his personal responsibility to rein it in. Beck knew he was the best hope for obtaining a warrant to search the secret facility. He often referred to himself as a champion of the people. A champion is what they needed.

Beck would much rather meet with the judge in person, but time was not on her side. A phone call would have to do. She gathered her thoughts and picked up the phone. After ringing briefly, a female voice came on the line. "Judge Wright's office."

"Good afternoon, I would like to speak with Judge Wright."

"The judge is not in his office right now. Would you like to make an appointment?"

"Do you expect him back in the office today?"

"He's in court right now. We expect him back later this afternoon."

"Could I leave him a message, please?"

"Yes, go ahead."

"My name is Rebecca Larmar. I'm an attorney who was once a student of his in law school. Please ask him to call me. It's very important."

"I'll see that he gets the message."

"Thank you."

"Goodbye."

Beck knew it was a long shot to catch him in his office right away, but that didn't dispel her frustration. It could be days before she received a call, or never. She got a cup of coffee and started thinking about what could happen if her plan to appeal to the judge didn't work. Thankfully, she didn't have to think for long.

Her phone rang, and her admin told her Judge Wright was on the line. She told the admin to put him through. "Hello, this is Rebecca Larmar."

"Rebecca, it's so good to hear from you. Please forgive my staff. They screen my calls, and your name was not on their list of callers to put through. I've corrected that. Your name is now on the list. How many years has it been since we talked?"

"I don't know for sure. Eight years at least."

"Has it been that long? Time seems to rush past me faster every year. You may not know this, but you were one of the best students I ever had."

"Thank you, Judge. That's very nice of you to say."

"I mean it. You were one student who understood what I was teaching."

"That's true, Judge. I took your lectures to heart."

"Your message said it was important. What can I do for you, young lady?"

Beck wasted no more time with pleasantries. She explained the situation, leaving out only the most extraneous information. She told him about Crease and Rose finding a structure in the deep woods. She also said they believed the structure drew the campers into the woods where they disappeared.

She also talked about Special Agent in Charge Tyrone Bevee. She began by telling the judge about the grudge Bevee had with Crease and continued by relating the story of the search of Crease's home. She concluded her narration about Bevee with the discovery of his fingerprints at the crime scene before he could have known anything about the disappearance.

Once she had told him everything, she requested a search warrant for the structure Rose saw deep in the forest. When she stopped talking, she heard nothing in response. After a few seconds, she said, "Judge, are you still there?"

"Yes, Rebecca, I'm sorry. I was busy taking notes. You believe this structure is a government facility, and it involves this Agent Bevee?"

"That is correct."

"If I grant you a search warrant, do you know how you would serve it?"

"Sheriff Broussard assured me if I got the warrant he would serve it."

"Based upon what you've told me, I'll grant you the search warrant. I'm afraid the people in that facility won't accept it. They're likely to believe they are not subject to the law. I wish you the best of luck."

"Thank you, Judge, I have confidence in Sheriff Broussard. He'll get the job done."

"All right, Rebecca, you've got it. Let's have your staff speak with my staff to work out the logistics. However this plays out, I'd like to hear from you again. You are on the accepted caller list now. Let me know how things are going for you once in a while."

"Yes, Judge, I'll do that."

"Excellent, Rebecca. It was wonderful to speak with you today. I'm going to transfer this call to my admin now."

"Goodbye, Judge, and thank you again."

Beck transferred the call to her assistant and explained what was going on. Despite her previous claim of confidence in Sheriff Mo, she had a feeling getting the warrant was the simple part.

Chapter 18

Crease was very glad to receive a call from Mo saying he was on his way to the courthouse to pick up the search warrant. It had been less than forty-eight hours since they had met with everyone, but Crease was wearing down. He hadn't been sleeping well before his two late-night friends paid him a visit. Now he was sleeping with one eye open, as they say, which meant he was sleeping hardly at all.

"How do you plan to serve the warrant?" Crease asked Mo on the phone.

"The problem is, to serve it we have to be there, to be there we have to get there, and we almost can't get there from here."

"As profound as that sounds, I'm not sure how it helps us."

"I'm working on a plan. We're going to need you to fly a floatplane. How many people can you transport at once?"

"Four is the max. Less if there's a lot of equipment."

"We're going to have more than that. I'll ask Pete if he'll fly a second plane."

"That would work."

"It's going to take some time for me to get everything together, but I don't want to wait long. Plan on meeting at the Outfitters tomorrow afternoon. Will that work?"

"I'll be there."

Sheriff Mo hadn't mentioned a specific time to meet at the Outfitters, so Crease packed up a few things and got over there early in the afternoon. He knew he must get the floatplanes checked and fueled up. He got that completed and went into the warehouse to pick up a couple of things.

It was midafternoon before Crease saw the sheriff's cruiser pull into the parking lot. It surprised him to see another vehicle coming in behind it. At first, that concerned him until he saw Tiny was driving the second vehicle. With him was another ample gentleman Crease had seen working at the Bobcat Bar and Grill.

Crease walked out to meet the sheriff as he was getting out of the cruiser. With the sheriff were Deputies Pride and Jensen. He told them the planes were ready to go. He walked to the back of the cruiser with the deputies to unload what they had brought along. Most of what he saw comprised firearms and related equipment. The number of firearms showed Crease the sheriff was expecting trouble.

One other item they carried to the planes was a large bolt cutter. That made him want to ask what the sheriff had in mind. He figured that would be discussed soon enough, however.

Once they had loaded everything, they all converged around the floatplanes. Crease said, "Okay, Sheriff, where are we going?"

"Let's head for Roudy's Cabin. Since we can't land a floatplane on that camouflaged landing area we saw beside that structure, I figured we'll stay in the cabin tonight and hike to it in the morning."

"That sounds like as good a plan as any other."

Ol' Pete came down from the Outfitters and took the pilot seat in the second floatplane. When everyone had loaded, Crease motioned to him to take off first. This was not an act of courtesy, but one of self-consciousness. Crease didn't want Pete watching him take off.

The flight to Roudy's Cabin was a quiet one. It seemed no one had much to say, or they were all lost in their own thoughts.

Crease eventually asked the sheriff, "I noticed you brought along some extra muscle. Are you going to deputize everybody?"

"Everyone but Pete. He's flying back after we unload. He told me he had done his share of hiking through jungles in Vietnam. I couldn't argue with that."

The flight went along without incident and when they arrived at the cabin site, the lake water was still. Crease radioed Pete to land first. Crease set down right after. They tied up at the dock and Crease went to get the ATV and trailer. They loaded everything onto the trailer and said their goodbyes to Ol' Pete, who wished them luck before taking off to fly back to the Outfitters.

The weather was agreeable. Not only was there no wind, but the temperature was almost balmy for the time of year. Mo had brought food along and suggested they build a fire in the pit and have a little campout. Everyone agreed that sounded like a good idea.

They got settled in and built a fire. Mo had packed hot dogs and marshmallows. Deputy Pride took the job of finding and crafting roasting sticks. Tiny had brought beer, which added to an already pleasant experience. It was only the thought of what might happen tomorrow that kept them from having a great time.

After they ate they sat around and watched the fire. Crease said, "I couldn't help but notice you asked Tiny and his friend to come along. What do you expect tomorrow, Mo?"

"I don't know what to expect, but I believe in being prepared for anything. Which reminds me, I need to ask if you've ever handled a gun before."

"Yes. Being a red-blooded, all-American Texas boy, I was raised around guns. I took a marksmanship course in college. I was the best shot in my class."

"I figured that would be the case, but I didn't want to wait until the shit hits the fan to find out."

"I saw the guns you brought along. I can handle all of them except maybe that big one. Is that a Browning Automatic Rifle?"

"Yes, it is. You don't see a BAR every day, but we confiscated that one during a drug bust."

"That ought to get the job done."

"Most jobs, yes, but I'd feel better if we also had a rocket-propelled grenade."

"You really know how to inspire confidence, don't you, Sheriff?"

"I don't like to sugarcoat things. I think if we are successful in executing that warrant without one or more of us being injured or worse, we will be very lucky."

"I understand that because I've been involved, but are

Tiny and company aware of what they are getting into?"

"They know. I wouldn't drag someone into this without explaining the dangers involved. Tiny enjoys doing deputy work. He likes arresting people."

"Really?"

"That's what he says. I've had to rein him in some because he sometimes got a little too enthusiastic about putting the cuffs on people. If they resisted at all, they were likely to end up with a cast."

"I'm hoping he gets the chance to do what he enjoys tomorrow, cast or not."

Chapter 19

Dawn broke early the next morning. Crease's mind was active before consciousness engulfed his body. It was busy working through recent events, looking for an explanation for his current situation. The answers it found were unsatisfying.

There was a real possibility he could face mortality before this day ended. That was a reality soldiers dealt with, not floatplane pilots. Even as he considered it, a small voice in his mind was telling him he didn't need to worry about that. It would never happen to him. It made him wonder if soldiers heard the same voice. Perhaps that was what allowed them to face dangerous situations.

It wasn't long before the blanket of consciousness covered him, and he noticed the sounds of the forest. Soon, sounds of his companions stirring covered those of the forest. The sheriff had included the makings of a hearty breakfast in the supplies brought along to support this endeavor. The smell of bacon brought the last of the party to life.

Deputy Jensen took full advantage of the kitchen in Roudy's Cabin. He showed himself to be quite a short-order cook. The company devoured the breakfast meal he prepared as if it might be their last meal. Crease suspected Tiny and his companion approached every meal that way.

Once the last scraps of bacon disappeared, Sheriff Mo gathered everyone together to explain his plan for the day. It was uncomplicated. They would hike north from the cabin, heading for the GPS coordinates Crease had recorded when circling the area. Once there, they would present the warrant and search the facility, arresting Agent Bevee if he was in attendance.

Crease listened until the sheriff asked if there were questions. "What is your plan B?"

Mo was firm when he answered. "Plan B isn't my concern. I didn't pack the arsenal of weapons for show. I intend to get into that structure. By force if necessary. If we fail, Plan B will be someone else's problem." Crease already knew that deep down, but hearing it stated as a fact was more than a little unsettling.

Everyone got dressed for the day, and Sheriff Mo distributed the rifles and handguns. He hung the bolt cutter from his pack and they began the trek to the secret government facility. They walked in a line so that clearing one path was all they needed.

Progress was still slow. The pine trees grew close together so that their limbs entangled. Below the entanglement grew shrubs, many with barbs or briars. The person in the front of the procession had to use a machete, taking two or three swings for each step in the thickest of the woods. Even though they were progressing slowly, the hike was exhausting. On the few occasions where they found a clearing, they stopped to gather strength.

When they came upon a small clearing where a large pine had fallen, they sat and rehydrated. After he had caught his breath, Crease said, "Mo, maybe we should have tried to find a chopper to fly us in."

"I gave it some thought, but I decided the element of surprise would be valuable to us. Now I'm wondering if I overthought it. Next time this situation comes up, we'll have the benefit of experience." That comment generated a little laughter. "Let's rest another ten minutes, and then we'll get moving again. I think we've got another two hours of hiking to do."

His estimate was fairly close. It was fifteen minutes short of two hours when Crease, who was walking in the lead, stopped and waved a hand to have everyone stop. Something caught his eye as he peered through the undergrowth. Mo crept up to see what had made him stop. Crease put his index finger across his lips to show the conversation needed to be hushed.

Mo whispered, "Do you see something?"

"Yes, just a glimpse of something, I don't know what, but it isn't trees or shrubs. Maybe fifty yards ahead. I thought we should stop and be quiet so we can look at what it is."

The sheriff nodded in agreement before creeping forward as quietly as possible through the thick brush. He had gone several yards when he stopped and crouched down. Everyone followed suit. There was a bit of an opening between the trees that allowed him to see most of what lay ahead.

What he saw was definitely a man-made facility.

Surprisingly small, because most of the building was underground. Cinder block walls made up the building that he could see. They had painted the walls with a camouflaged pattern that blended into the forest. There was one door and the back of the building sloped down, no doubt to cover the stairway to the underground facility.

An eight-foot chain-link fence enclosed the small structure. They had affixed razor wire to the top of the fence. The gate in the fence was chained closed. On either side of the ten-foot gate were small, square guard posts, not over three feet square, with a pitched roof that was also camouflaged. Mounted on the guard posts and the building were cameras that peered at the gate and into the forest. A metal sign attached to the gate read: *Access to this area is forbidden. Use of deadly force is authorized.*

Crease and the party quietly moved closer to the facility. There was at least one guard inside the fence. Off to the left, outside the fence, Crease noticed the landing area they saw on the satellite images. It was a small clearing in the trees but not cleared of shrubs and brush. A helicopter could land there, but from the air, it would look like the forest.

Sheriff Mo whispered to everyone to spread out and move behind him toward the facility. They all did as the sheriff had asked. Mo crept forward slowly until he was behind the last set of trees and brush outside the gate.

Crease edged closer to the sheriff and said, "What's the plan, Sheriff?"

"Now that everyone is in position to cover me, I'm going to go tell that guard why we're here and that I expect him to open the gate."

"That has the virtue of being simple, I guess."

"Look at it this way. We're on the right side of this. We have a valid warrant to enter that facility. If they refuse, then we are in the right to enforce it."

"It's that enforce part that makes me nervous."

"Yeah, me, too, but here we go."

The sheriff gave his rifle to Crease so he wouldn't appear threatening as he moved to the gate. He believed what he read on the sign and didn't want to push his luck. He stood and plodded toward the gate and the visible guard.

At first, his movement went unnoticed by the guard, but when Mo stepped on a twig that snapped, the guard turned to identify the sound. When he saw the sheriff standing by the gate, it didn't seem to register in his mind right away. Mo suspected they didn't get many unexpected visitors.

"Stand right there and don't move." The guard pointed an M4 carbine toward the sheriff. "This entire area is off-limits. Stay right where you are while I report this."

The sheriff said, "I'm Sheriff Maurice Broussard, and I have a federal warrant to enter and search this facility." As he said that he held up the warrant so the guard could see it.

The guard stepped to the little guard post and picked up a phone receiver. Underground, inside the building, a security wall phone rang. An agent standing close by answered it. "Who? You're kidding. Hold on and I'll get SAC Bevee."

Bevee was the special agent in charge, but he did most of his work in his office miles from this lab. He had flown in two days ago to review some results in person. From across the room, the agent holding the phone waved at him to approach. Bevee walked over, expecting some routine issue to be the reason he was needed. The agent holding the phone handed it to Bevee and said, "We have a situation at the front gate."

"This is SAC Bevee."

"Sir, a Sheriff Broussard is here, and he claims to have a search warrant."

"Son of a bitch!" Bevee hadn't heard of any legal wrangling going on in the background. He thought Williams and Broussard finally got the message to stand down. At least he had hoped that was the case. "I'm coming up. Keep him where he is."

As Bevee made his way up to the front gate, he grabbed his satellite phone and called the assistant director. He walked and talked at the same time. After he explained the situation, the AD replied, "I thought you had everything under control."

"I did. I don't know how they could have gotten a warrant."

"Keep him out of that facility and keep this line open so I can hear what's going on."

"Yes, sir."

Agent Bevee came out of the door on the front of the building but didn't move closer to the gate. A few seconds later, three agents came out of the door and fanned out across the fenced-in area. Each of them carried an M4 rifle. Agent Bevee told them to stay alert.

Bevee then called out, "What are you doing here, Sheriff?"

"I've got a search warrant for this property. Besides that, I'm going to arrest you for theft and planting evidence."

"You have self-confidence. I'll give you that, Sheriff. You aren't coming in here and I'm not leaving with you."

"I've got a federal warrant that says I can come in. I

intend to serve it and enforce it if necessary. I've got armed deputies along the tree line."

Crease and the others moved out from behind their trees so Agent Bevee could see them. Bevee appeared a bit surprised to see the five well-armed men with Crease among them.

"It doesn't matter, Sheriff. We're not opening the gate, so you may as well go back where you came from."

"You are defying a federal order. We're coming in. If you don't remove that padlock and chain, I came prepared to do it for you."

Bevee raised his voice so that everyone in the area could hear. "Agents, if anyone touches that lock, shoot them down."

Mo stood, staring at Bevee as if frozen in place. Then he said, "Any blood that gets shed here today is on you."

Bevee still held the satellite phone connected to his assistant director, but it remained silent. A vile grin appeared on his face and he said, "I won't lose any sleep over it. You are in way over your head, Sheriff. Go back home."

Mo began backing up toward Crease, who held the bolt cutter. He didn't turn his back to Bevee as he went. When he got within arm's reach of Crease, he turned to face him. They moved behind the trees, and Crease said, "Damn, Mo, what's your plan now?"

"I'm gonna cut that chain off." Mo took the bolt cutter from Crease.

"Sheriff, I don't think Bevee is bluffing. They will open fire if you touch that lock."

"You may be right, but what is the alternative? We pack up and leave, then what? Wait for them to come to visit you in the night again? Let them destroy my life? We have to continue. The law is on our side."

"Is that what you want on your tombstone? *The law is on our side.*"

"Let's hope it doesn't come to that. It's no use continuing to talk about it. I'm going to go cut that chain, God help me. If they open up on me, shoot back. Cover me if you can."

Crease grabbed Mo's arm and pulled him close. "You can't do this. I'm the one who got this whole thing started. This is just as much my fight as is it yours. You've got a family to think about. I don't. I couldn't face your wife knowing I let you do this."

"It's my job—"

"It's mine too. You deputized me. I'm an officer of the law. I'm also the one Bevee wants to get even with. There's something else too, Mo. I haven't told many people this, but I don't have many years to live."

"What are you talking about?"

"I've known it for a long time. It's the reason I keep people at arm's length. I found out after a DNA test in college. I'm not bullshitting you. I'd much rather go out like this, doing something meaningful, than slowly wasting away. If they shoot me, you make sure they pay for it, okay?"

Mo hesitated, but he handed the bolt cutter to Crease, who now had the bolt cutter in one hand and a 9mm handgun in the other. He looked out at the gate and figured it to be maybe thirty feet away. Could he run for it? He knew that wouldn't work. It might even startle the nervous guards into shooting before he got there. No, slow and steady was the only way to do it.

"Make me a promise, Mo."

"Anything."

"If this doesn't go well, will you look after Beck? Keep her safe and make sure she ends up with a good man. Someone who is worthy of her."

"You have my word, my friend."

He took a long breath and looked at the gate. Thirty feet away. He wondered how far convicts had to walk to the gallows. What he was feeling must be pretty close to the way they felt.

He started slowly walking out of the trees and toward the gate. Thoughts rushed through his mind as he took each step. Would Beck hate him for this after his death? He couldn't decide. He figured it mattered little either way. He'd never know about it. When he was about twenty feet away, it occurred to him what a beautiful day this was. How many days had passed without his notice in the last ten years? Not all, perhaps, but most of them. He realized how he'd been living in a fog. He'd just been allowing life to pass by.

When he had stepped within ten feet of the gate, a sound caught his attention. It was the sound of the guards raising their rifles to aim. He could have done without that. When it sank in that they were aiming at him, a thought struck him like a lightning bolt. It made him stop in his tracks. Beck had been right. She said you can't live your life based on what you think might happen. He'd been sure all these years what his fate was going to be, a slow, lingering death because of Alzheimer's. Yet here he was, about to die, and it had nothing to do with disease. He suppressed a sudden urge to laugh. He wished he could tell her, but it was too late for that.

He was ten feet away and the time for regrets was over. He took a step forward when another sound made him pause. Not the sound of guards like before. This was a sound off in the distance, a sound that didn't belong out here in the forest.

Sheriff Mo heard the sound, too, and he had heard the sound before. It was a Huey, a helicopter used for many years by the military, but not these days. He raised his eyes toward the sky to see where it was.

As he looked up to find the source of the sound, Crease realized the guards were no longer looking at him. They were looking for the sound as well. It got louder as the seconds ticked by. Then it was there, hanging in the air just to the east. Crease noticed it was larger than the helicopters used by hospitals for emergency transport.

Mo saw it and couldn't believe what he was seeing. It was a Huey all right. It looked like it was coming right out of a battle in Vietnam. It was army green and both side doors were wide open. The only thing missing were the .50-caliber machine guns on both sides. For a moment, he was disappointed about that.

The chopper swung around and hovered over the camouflaged landing area before slowly easing to the ground. When it landed, people jumped out from both side doors. They carried microphones and video cameras. The reporters wore jackets with their station names and call letters embroidered on the front.

At first, Crease didn't know how to react. Then he looked over to where Bevee was standing with his satellite phone. He had the phone to his ear and was listening with a devastated look on his face.

"Yes sir. A chopper filled with news people. It just landed. They are swarming around setting up equipment at this moment."

"Damn it, Bevee, you've failed this project. Tell your men to hold their fire. We can't refuse the warrant with reporters looking on. Open the gate for them, Bevee. We can expect a lot of questions after this, and a lot of fingers pointing. Prepare yourself. Most of the fingers are going to be pointing at you. All we can do now with the press looking on is cooperate with the sheriff. Hang up and go do that. Don't make this any worse than it is already."

Bevee closed his eyes, rubbed his forehead, and replied with a weak, "Yes sir." He then put the phone down and did what he was told. He walked to one of the small guard posts and got the key to the lock. Crease watched as he plodded to the gate and removed the chain. He told the other agents to lower their weapons.

Sheriff Mo came out from behind cover and motioned to the deputies to do the same. They all converged around Crease, standing just outside the now open gate. Crease looked at Mo and saw he was staring at the Huey. Crease turned to see what he was staring at when out from the pilot's seat, dressed in vintage Vietnam-era fatigues, came Ol' Pete.

Pete walked through all the reporters and camera operators to get to Crease and Mo. With a big grin on his face, he said, "I hated leaving you guys to do this alone, so I thought I'd bring you some company. I called every news outlet I could find within a fifty-mile radius. I told 'em all what was going on up here and that there was only one way in and out, and that was with me. I had to leave some of them back in town. Couldn't fit 'em all in."

Crease said, "I've never had the urge to kiss you until just now."

"Woah there, junior, let's not get carried away."

Sheriff Mo said, "Pete! Where the hell did you get that thing?"

"Ain't she a beauty? A buddy of mine back in Nam used to fly one. A few years ago he bought her from army surplus when she was decommissioned. He took the time to restore her back to flying condition. When I told him what you guys were doing up here, he was happy to let me borrow her for a couple of days."

Mo said, "You are a sight for sore eyes. I can't believe you came up with this wild idea on your own, but I'm grateful you did."

"I've had a few bright ideas in my time. I really just wanted an excuse to fly the Huey." Pete smiled as he said that.

Just then, one reporter made his way to Sheriff Mo and began asking questions. Mo told him, "We are going to search this site. When we come back out, I'll provide a statement and answer questions."

The sheriff turned to his assembled deputies and said, "Gentlemen, let's do what we came here for."

Mo led the group through the gate but stopped at the small guard post where Agent Bevee was standing. The sheriff turned to Tiny and handed him a set of handcuffs. "Please put Special Agent in Charge Bevee under arrest."

Tiny took the cuffs and told Bevee to turn around slowly and put his hands behind his back. As he was about to cuff him, Tiny said, "Don't struggle around too much. That's how things get broken." Tiny told Bevee to sit down on the ground and not to move.

Crease, Sheriff Mo, and Deputy Pride headed for the door of the facility and left Tiny and the others to keep order outside. Considering all the trouble it had caused, the inside of the facility was unremarkable. The room that sat above ground was empty except for one small desk and chair. On the backside of the room, there was a doorway that led down a wide flight of stairs. The bottom of the stairs opened into the underground laboratory.

Along one wall of the lab were doors that led into small offices. The main room of the lab contained various types of equipment and measuring devices. It wasn't remarkably different from a college physics lab. Most of the equipment wasn't readily identifiable. Based upon the labels and some of the measuring devices, it was clear the primary focus of the lab was weapons development. Ol' Pete had been correct in his prediction. Much of the equipment appeared to be devoted to electromagnetic pulse testing.

There were people in the lab, technicians mostly. No one offered any resistance as Crease and the others moved through the lab. On the back wall of the main lab was a double door that led into another lab area. Along one wall of this second room were doors that led to living areas, much like army barracks. There was also a kitchen and a small dining area. Crease marveled at the effort it must have taken to create this facility so far out in the forest.

On the back wall of this second large lab was a single door that led to a hallway with restrooms and storage areas. At the end of the hallway, a door on one side looked out of place. It looked like the standard door had been replaced with one made of reinforced steel with a large through bolt to keep it closed.

Crease was apprehensive as he reached for the bolt to unlock the door. He disengaged the bolt and opened the door. Inside was a small, makeshift prison cell. They had converted the room for that purpose. Crease recognized the four men fearfully waiting inside as the campers he had flown to Roudy's Cabin. One man spoke up and said, "Look, guys, that's the pilot that flew us to the cabin. Oh my God, it's good to see you!"

The men all began hugging Crease, Mo, and Deputy Pride and thanking them for coming to their rescue. After the initial exuberance had settled down, Crease said, "What happened? How did you guys get locked up?"

"It was my fault," one camper said. "I saw this place one evening, but it was getting dark. I thought it was some kind of abandoned building. I talked everyone into coming back the next day. When we got here, the gate was open, and no one was outside. We walked on in before we realized it wasn't abandoned. When they saw us, we were lucky they didn't shoot us on sight. They locked us in here and interrogated us. They thought we were spies. When they asked if we had told anyone about this place, I told them I had put an entry in my daily journal. It wasn't long after that they created this cell to keep us in. They said they had too much invested in this place to allow it to be discovered. One guard told us they were only keeping us alive until they knew no one would look for us anymore. You guys are lifesavers."

Crease realized Bevee's plan was to try him for the disappearances, then when it was over, he would dispose of these guys. He found it hard to believe how far he would go to keep this place secret.

Sheriff Mo led everyone out of the lab and made a brief statement to the press. It took a while for the reporters to talk to everyone who would say anything. It took Ol' Pete a couple of trips in the Huey to get everyone back to civilization. Mo locked Bevee up and charged him with kidnapping, among other crimes.

Chapter 20

The story of the secret weapons lab hidden in the thick forest was all over the news for a few days. Reporters billed the incarceration of the four campers and the attempted coverup as a glaring example of a government agency run amok. Government officials claimed the ugly mess was all the work of one midlevel official with delusions of grandeur.

Special Agent in Charge Tyrone Bevee shouldered the blame, believing that made him patriotic somehow. He would eventually testify before a Senate subcommittee formed to investigate the debacle. Once he completed his testimony, he made some appearances on television news programs. His notoriety faded with time and he disappeared from public view. His whereabouts are currently unknown.

The federal government removed all evidence of weapons development from the secret lab and deeded the property to the state of Minnesota. They built a lookout tower on the site and turned it into a forest ranger station.

Maurice Broussard ran for reelection as county sheriff. He was unopposed. He made regular appearances on stage at the Bobcat Bar and Grill, sitting in at the piano with various jazz bands who came to play.

For several weeks, conversations in any local bar, barbershop, or waiting room focused on the events that transpired in the deep woods. Everyone had their own opinion, and the stories grew more dramatic with each retelling. Gradually, stories became less frequent, and daily life returned to normal. There were a few notable exceptions.

Crease was having his regular weekly coffee at Perks Your Interest. In the door walked Gina Owens with her daughter, Christina. When she saw Crease sitting at his table, Christina ran to him, saying, "Mr. Crease, Mr. Crease, do you see? I don't need my wheelchair anymore." She stopped in front of him and spun around in a circle.

"Look at you. That is wonderful!"

"She couldn't wait until you came into the store to show you," Gina said. "I knew you came here for coffee about this time, so we stopped by."

"I'm thrilled you did. It's great to see her on her feet."

Gina and Christina waved goodbye and left the coffee shop just before Beck came in. She embraced Crease and gave him a kiss. It had become well-known that they were a couple, and they spent every spare moment together.

The experience was an eye-opening one for Crease. He realized life is precious and precarious. It is short for everyone—for him shorter than most—and more than anything else, he wanted to spend the rest of it with Beck, for better or worse.

Looking back on it, Crease realized finding the four missing campers and returning them safely to their families gave him a great deal of satisfaction. It was the silver lining to an otherwise dark and gloomy cloud of an experience. It had been a lot of trouble, with the arrest, the threats, and the fear of being shot dead in the woods, but he felt a sense of accomplishment for the first time since his college days. More than that, he had found the love of his life.

What better ending to his career as a crime solver could he ask for? He was happy to return to his life as a washed-up football player turned float-plane pilot. He'd leave the crime-solving to the professionals. At least, that was his plan. Then came the day Gerald Becker brought his daughter Sidney into the sheriff's office.

Made in the USA
Middletown, DE
19 May 2022

65899259R00111